B.Y. High

Making Her Mark

Created by **Miriam Dombey** • Written by **Perel Schreiber**

B.Y. High

Making Her Mark

2

MENUCHA PUBLISHERS

Menucha Publishers, Inc.
First published 1994
© 2023 by Menucha Publishers
All rights reserved

ISBN 978-1-61465-891-7
Library of Congress Control Number: 2023933387

Published and distributed by:
Menucha Publishers, Inc.
1235 38th Street
Brooklyn, NY 11218
Tel/Fax: 718-232-0856
www.menuchapublishers.com
sales@menuchapublishers.com

Printed in Israel

One

The sky was a dreary shade of gray, with gloomy snowflakes drifting sluggishly through the freezing air as winter locked the small town of Bloomfield in icy patterns of frost. The cold wind blew insistently against the closed windows of the Bais Yaakov building, rattling dead leaves across the blacktop. The sturdy building, however, stood indifferently against the wind's onslaught, its red brick walls impervious to snow and ice.

Those inhabiting the building weren't quite so impassive about the howling wind and insistent snow. The students of Bais Yaakov of Bloomfield, from the smallest first grader to the ninth graders of the fledgling high school, huddled into their desks, the expressions on their faces mirroring the unpleasant weather outside.

In such weather, a teacher's voice sounds more dron-
ing, more boring, and the homework and tests seem
incredibly more difficult. The girls shifted restlessly in
their seats, edgy and uncomfortable with everything
and nothing at the same time. Shani Baum, sitting in
the ninth-grade classroom in the row closest to the
window, was no exception.

Shani eyed the swirling snowflakes morosely. School
is bad enough during ordinary weather. It's worse when
the air is warm and fresh with spring, and you have to
sit indoors in class when little green buds are breaking
through the damp earth to shyly raise their heads to the
sunlight. But when the weather is stormy enough and
miserable enough to make you want to pull the covers
over your head and stay in bed until sometime in mid-
April... Even the teachers looked depressed. Who could
possibly pay attention to *dikduk* on a day like this?

With an effort, Shani pulled her gaze away from
the mesmerizing sight of snow and dirty slush piled
outside the window. With the weather so blustery, she
knew it was inevitable that they would have another
day of recess indoors. Indoor recess, cooped up in the
somewhat drafty gym with the rest of the school.

Not that spending recess with the rest of the school
was all that terrible...

Shani smiled to herself as she absentmindedly tugged
at the crisp pleats of her uniform skirt. At first, the idea

of doing anything together with the younger classes had seemed demeaning, almost horrifying. They were high school girls, weren't they? Shouldn't they be separate, different? It had taken her and the rest of the ninth grade some time to see that with their status as high school students, they had a definite role to play in Bais Yaakov of Bloomfield: the older girls, able to lead and show the way. And with their new, neat uniforms of yellow and blue plaid, so unlike the navy skirt and light blue blouses that made up the dress code of the elementary school, they all stood out as something special.

It was a challenge, certainly. As Rebbetzin Falovitz, the high school's beloved principal, was so fond of saying, "No privilege comes without responsibility!" But Shani, together with the rest of the ninth-grade class — both the native Bloomfielders and the five boarders from out-of-town — were ready, willing, and eager to accept the challenge.

Shani started out of her reverie as the bell rang, signaling the end of class and the beginning of recess. With murmurs of relief, the ninth graders closed their notebooks, stood up, and stretched. Snacks materialized from nowhere, and the girls began to drift out of the classroom and into the hall, gathering into small groups as they laughed and chatted.

Shani, escaping the classroom with a strong feeling of relief, found herself walking next to Raizy Segal.

Raizy! It was hard to believe that only a year ago, Raizy had been shy and quiet, the "class genius" that nobody really knew. Shani often thought that it was a real pity she'd wasted all those years in school together, ignoring "colorless" Raizy who just didn't seem interesting at all...

The thick-lensed glasses that had partially hidden Raizy's face were gone now, replaced by soft contact lenses; and she'd abandoned her utilitarian ponytail for a short, blunt cut that framed her thin face attractively. But the transformation was more than that: Raizy's eyes shone with quiet confidence, and her easy smile reflected the wry sense of humor that she usually kept under wraps. Shani knew she'd been partially instrumental in letting Raizy blossom, but she also knew that Raizy had helped *her* to grow and mature in the last year as well.

"This weather is terrible," Shani complained to the taller girl as the two of them strolled down the hallway toward the gym.

Raizy smiled at her ruefully. "I know. We'll just have to make the best of it."

"I suppose so..." Shani shook her head with irritation, ruffling her blond hair. "But how am I supposed to concentrate on anything in weather like this?"

Raizy shrugged her shoulders, a rueful smile tugging at the corners of her mouth. "Think of something else."

"Like what?" Shani perked up a little, a tinge of interest coloring her voice. "Is something going on that I don't know about?"

"No, not really," Raizy replied in her soft voice. A thoughtful expression crossed her face. "You know something? Maybe that's the problem…"

Shani blinked. "What do you mean?"

Chaya Samet, walking nearby, overheard Raizy's remark. She quickly stepped forward, her brown eyes dark with intensity. "I'll tell you what Raizy means," she declared, her voice carrying a trace of petulance. "Nothing's happening these days. Chanukah was over a week ago, and there's absolutely nothing to look forward to."

"You have a point," Shani said thoughtfully. Her blue eyes sparkled with sudden excitement. "So let's do something!"

"Yeah?" Chaya looked skeptical. "What do you have in mind?"

"What if we make some kind of performance?" Shani suggested. "That should break up the monotony."

"Like what?" Chaya countered, a frown creeping over her normally pleasant expression. "The elementary just put on their play Chanukah time. We can't do that. And they had a carnival, too. We can't do that either…"

"We participated in that carnival," Raizy reminded her mildly. "Remember?"

"Yeah, but we just ran a few booths." Chaya scowled. "The elementary ruins all the good ideas."

"What's that supposed to mean?" Shani demanded, feeling a flush of annoyance warm her cheeks. Was Chaya going to start up that old, worn-out argument again about how horrible it was to be stuck together with the elementary classes?

Apparently, yes. "You know what I mean," Chaya grumbled. "Every time we want to come up with some idea for an activity, it's already taken by the elementary. If we wouldn't be stuck together with them, we wouldn't have such a hard time coming up with something to do!"

Shani opened her mouth to protest, but she was interrupted. "That's right," chimed in Chana Hochberg, coming up alongside Raizy. "Michal and I were talking about making a choir, but the play the elementary just put on was a musical. Nobody's going to be interested in a choir now."

Shani groaned inwardly. Why did they have to keep rehashing the same tired phrases over and over again? Perhaps there *were* some disadvantages to being in the same school with the elementary, but that didn't mean the girls couldn't go ahead and do something different of their own. Why waste time and energy with senseless complaining?

Raizy, with that uncanny sense of hers, seemed to read Shani's mind. "I'll tell you what, Chana," she suggested. "Let's do something different. Hmm… I know! Let's make a band choir instead."

"A band choir?" Chana, the ninth grade's band leader, looked interested, the peevish expression of a moment before fading away. "What's that?"

"I mean that the main thing should be the music, not the singing. The singing should accompany the music and not the other way around."

"How will that help us?" Chaya asked sullenly. "It's still a choir when you get right down to it."

"Not really," broke in Shani, her voice charged with sudden excitement. "Think about it, Chaya. Do you realize how many instruments we have?"

Chaya looked thoughtful. Chana grew exuberant, doing a little skip and dance as the idea caught fire.

"You're right, Raizy!" she exclaimed. "I play the piano, Suri plays the drums, Shoshanah has a triangle…"

"Bayla plays the guitar," Raizy added, smiling.

"And Elisheva plays the flute!" Shani finished, triumphant. "You're right, Raizy. A band choir is a great idea!" She whirled on Chaya. "You see? We *can* do different things when we want to!"

Chaya frowned a little. "That's true, but…"

"But what?" pressed Chana, caught by the idea and lost in a fond daydream where she and the other members of the high school band bowed to tumultuous applause. "What's the problem?"

"Oh, nothing. Nothing." Chaya forced a smile to her lips and walked a little ahead of the others. "That *is* a nice idea, I guess. But — well, it's still a choir."

"Ummm." Raizy looked thoughtful. "What troubles you, Chaya? That it's still a choir and not that special — or that it's like the elementary's performance?"

Chaya's shoulders slumped. She turned and looked back at the others, her smile turning sheepish. "I guess I'm being a little silly, huh?"

"It's okay," Shani quipped with a grin. "We're all entitled to be silly sometimes."

Chaya flashed her friend a grateful look. Shani's opinions meant a lot to her, as they did to the rest of the ninth graders. A natural leader, Shani seemed to radiate confidence and practicality, and her fellow classmates valued her judgment.

"Besides," Chana added, a little of her excitement leaking away, "you're not really being all that silly, Chaya. I feel that way sometimes, too…"

The noise level in the hall rose as the foursome neared the gym, and shouts and giggles provided a peculiar background music to their conversation. Chana tugged at one ear in annoyance. "See, that's exactly what I mean. I'll bet a high school, a real high school in New York, isn't as noisy as this!"

A sudden burst of laughter sent Chana spinning around to face a tall, broad-shouldered girl with a liberal sprinkling of freckles dotting her face and brown eyes glinting with cynical amusement. "Where did you ever get that idea?" Rochel Kaplan demanded.

With Chana's fair coloring, the flush on her cheeks was painfully obvious. "Well…"

Rochel rolled her eyes. "Believe me, Chana. There are more girls in a Boro Park high school than in this entire elementary *plus* high school combined. Trust me, it's noisy."

"Oh."

"Hello, Rochel," Shani said mildly, looking her boarder directly in the eye.

"Hello, Shani." Rochel grinned back. The others might not have understood what Shani meant by that hello, but Rochel did: *Rochel, we all know you're a Boro Parker. Don't take it out on us poor rustic Bloomfielders.*

Most of the ninth graders were more than a little intimidated by Rochel Kaplan. One of five boarders that had joined the new high school class in Bloomfield, Rochel was the only one coming from Brooklyn instead of a smaller community. She'd arrived with a king-sized chip on her shoulder, determined to do her very best to hate life in Bloomfield, and after a few awkward encounters, most of the girls had been more than willing to leave Rochel alone.

But Shani, who served as hostess to Rochel and the two other out-of-towners boarding in the basement of the Baum home, had broken past the fierce facade with which Rochel protected the painful emotions lurking just beneath the surface. She knew the bitter secret that Rochel kept locked up tightly within her, and she had learned to understand Rochel's particularly sardonic brand of humor.

Raizy glanced quickly from Chana to Rochel. "We were just talking about making a band choir," she told Rochel, smoothly moving past the awkward moment of Chana's embarrassment. "We have such an interesting combination of instruments, especially since Elisheva is so talented at playing the flute. What do you think?"

Rochel, who couldn't help respecting Raizy for her frank common sense and quiet intelligence, favored her with a smile untinged by its usual sarcasm. "That sounds like a nice idea, Raizy. Trying to think of something to keep the winter blues away?"

"That's the general idea," chuckled Shani. "This weather is enough to turn anyone blue — with cold."

"Very funny." Rochel rolled her eyes.

"I also think it's a good idea," Chana declared, her momentary embarrassment overcome. "We've got the piano, the guitar, the drums, a triangle, *and* Elisheva's flute. It'll be great!"

Chaya coughed. Shani turned to her, frowning slightly.

"What's bothering you, Chaya?"

"Oh, nothing. Nothing."

"No, Shani's right." Raizy's forehead puckered, and she took a step forward, her brown eyes intent. "Something's troubling you, Chaya. What is it?"

"I don't want to say anything, but…"

"But what?" Rochel demanded. Chaya bit her lip and drew back a little.

"But what?" Shani repeated, more softly than Rochel but her voice still insistent.

"Well, I was just thinking…maybe it won't really work out all that well."

"What won't?"

"Making a band choir…"

"Why not?" Chana demanded. "*I* like the idea. I think it'll work."

"Well, of course you do," teased Raizy. "You're the band leader."

"So what?" Chana stuck her chin out belligerently. "What's wrong, Chaya? Why won't it work?"

"Well…" Chaya looked a little embarrassed. "You all know what kind of music Elisheva plays."

They all looked at Shani.

Elisheva Conrad was one of the three girls boarding at Shani's home. A South African native, her soft-spoken ways and lilting accent set her apart from the others. She was a talented musician, spending at least half an hour each day practicing her music, but…

"That's true," Chana agreed with forced reluctance. "I don't think anyone in Bais Yaakov is really interested in listening to classical music."

Rochel pressed her lips together into a thin, irritated line. At first, spending half an hour every day listening to Elisheva's classical music had driven her absolutely crazy. After a while, though, the sweet strains of Mozart and Chopin had begun to grow on her. She still wasn't all that enthused about classical music, but it was certainly not as terrible as Chana and Chaya were saying.

"Elisheva isn't stupid." Rochel's voice dripped scorn. "If she's playing with the rest of you, she's not gonna go and do her own thing. She'll play whatever music you tell her to." She turned away, disgusted. "Why don't you give her a little credit for intelligence?"

Chaya and Chana turned bright red. Shani, frowning, took two quick steps and grabbed Rochel by the arm.

"Don't you think you're overdoing it a little?" she suggested firmly, her voice frosting over.

Rochel blinked, then relaxed into a sheepish grin. "Yeah, Shani, you're right." She glanced over Shani's shoulder at the other girls. "Sorry."

Chaya held her head up high. "No problem," she said stiffly. She looked away.

Once again, Raizy stepped in and changed the subject. "One thing's for sure — it'll take a lot of hard work.

The music will really have to be special." She tapped her cheek thoughtfully. "Why don't we go to Rebbetzin Falovitz and get permission for this? Maybe we could make a performance on Tu B'Shevat…"

"We're making a 'Fruit Fiesta' then," Shani reminded her.

"Okay, so we'll make it some other time. Why not?"

"That's an idea," Chana agreed, cheering up again. "C'mon, Raizy. Let's go discuss it!"

Chaya, Chana, and Raizy walked off, heading toward the office and leaving Shani and Rochel alone.

Shani eyed her boarder with a twisted smile. "You really know how to win people over, Rochel, don't you?"

Rochel chuckled, the sound overlaid with a tinge of bitterness. "Some people are more talented than others, that's all." She shrugged her shoulders, as if dismissing the issue as unimportant, and looked away toward the lunchroom, where a group of second graders were busily playing together. Her eyes sought out one face, a serious little face with big brown eyes that held a deep and infinite sorrow…

"You don't have to be, you know," Shani pointed out, her voice gentle.

Rochel turned back to Shani and regarded her steadily, her eyes turning haunted. "Oh, yes, Shani," she disagreed, her voice a little sad now. "I do." Without another word, she turned and walked away.

Two

Shani sighed as she watched her boarder join the crowd of second graders, stooping over and talking to one particular child. Rochel was so sardonic, so sarcastic; but how could she blame her? Had she herself, *chas v'shalom*, gone through what Rochel had suffered, what would her own behavior be like...?

She thought back to the day several weeks ago, when Rochel had finally told her the truth: her father had died when she was in fifth grade, and her mother had recently remarried. She probably never would have told her anything at all — the others still didn't know anything about it — but Shani had been witness to the shocking scene with little Adina Newman, the second grader who had lost her father in a traffic accident. Images flashed through Shani's mind of that heart-rending incident in the second-grade classroom, when Adina had come back to school for the first time since her father's death, and Rochel had forced her to face the truth...

Adina jumped out of her chair and pointed a trembling finger at the chalkboard...at the refuah sheleimah chart, where her father's name had been written for five long weeks. Now the name was erased...gone. "Someone erased my Tatty's name! Put it back! Write it! Write it!"
... Rochel bent and picked Adina up. Adina struggled wildly... Rochel pinned down the flailing arms with her right hand, then cupped Adina's chin in her left hand and turned her head toward her, forcing the little girl to look at her. "Adina...we don't have to daven for your Tatty anymore...your Tatty is davening for us in shamayim... your Tatty is davening for us....your Tatty is davening for us...your Tatty is dav —"

"Shani?"

"What?" Shani blinked herself back into focus.

"Hey, Shani, wake up!" Tamar Bergman, her dark eyes sparkling with mischief, wagged a chiding finger. "You were totally spaced out. What's up?"

Shani relaxed and smiled. Tamar was the third boarder at the Baums' home. She hailed from the tiny town of Kedzie, Illinois, and she and Rochel were as different as...as...well, as different as Rochel and

Elisheva were — and Elisheva and Tamar, for that matter. "What makes you think something's up, Tamar?"

"Oh, I dunno." Tamar shrugged and grinned.
"Something in the air, I suppose."

"Besides all the snow?"

Tamar glanced at the window at the end of the hall.
The snowflakes swirled down faster than ever, a fierce,
grayish-white swirl to mask the gray clouds above. "A
snowball fight, maybe?" she suggested, her smile impish. Then she laughed. "Although that doesn't fit the
polished 'high school' image we ninth graders have to
project." She paused. "It's a pity, though," she added.

"Only you would think so, Tamar," Shani said with
a smile, her voice teasing.

"Oh, I'm not so sure about that," Tamar mused.
"There might be one or two other ninth graders like
me who don't mind getting their hands a little dirty…"
*Who wouldn't mind just having a good time, without
worrying whether it was "mature" or not…* But most of
the girls of the new B.Y. High were still anxious about
their image. Was Tamar the only one who really wanted
to plunge into life, to laugh and to sing and to experience the joy of helping others grow?

Tamar enjoyed the experience of living in the "big
city" of Bloomfield. It was certainly a far cry from her
home town, where so many of the Jewish families were
still learning about Yiddishkeit. But she couldn't help

missing the role she had played back in Kedzie: the rabbi's daughter, an integral part of the community with her own special job. Even now, after months in Bloomfield, she still felt a sharp pang at odd moments for the life she'd left behind: the cheeky fifth graders she'd helped to nurture and grow, the *shiurim* and classes she'd helped her mother organize, the knowledge that she, too, was a part of everything that happened...

"And here you were just teasing *me* about spacing out!"

Tamar started, letting Kedzie fade into the background as she lifted her head to meet Shani's blue gaze. "What's on your mind, Tamar?"

"Oh, nothing much," Tamar replied vaguely. She gave Shani an abstracted smile before wandering down the hallway and entering the noisy gym.

This is what she'd been missing. She looked around at the large room filled with girls, all concentrating on playing hard. She leaned against the wall, watching the younger girls idly. Here and there, she spotted a flash of yellow and blue plaid: one of the ninth graders, wending her sedate way through the teeming mass of blue skirts and light-blue blouses. They may have looked more mature, but they sure didn't look like they were having very much fun...

A sudden shriek sent her spinning around in time to see a blue *machanayim* ball on a direct collision course with her nose. Automatically, without even thinking about it, Tamar's hands shot up to catch the ball with a jarring thump. Her eyes sought out a group of girls gawking at her with surprise; fourth or fifth graders, from the look of them. With a mischievous grin, her dark eyes alive with amusement, she reached back and threw the ball with all the force she could muster, slamming it directly into one of the watching girls.

"You're out!" she called over the noise, loud enough for them to hear.

The girl, whose face had momentarily worn a look of indignation, relaxed and giggled. She came over to where Tamar was standing.

"You're Tamar Bergman, aren't you?" she asked a little shyly.

"I sure am." Tamar grinned at her disarmingly. Nobody knew how to make a younger girl feel at ease better than she did. "Who's been telling on me?"

"Oh, nobody." The girl grinned back. "But I know you're not from Bloomfield, so you're either Rochel Kaplan or Batsheva Teitelbaum or Elisheva Conrad or Tamar Bergman or Rivka Pollack."

"Well, that's true." Tamar crossed her ankles and leaned back against the wall. "How do you know all the out-of-towners' names?"

By now, several of the others had come drifting forward to gather around Tamar. "We got this whole pamphlet at the beginning of the year," one of them, a girl with mousy brown braids, volunteered. "It had a whole list of the ninth-grade class, plus a 'welcome' page for the out-of-towners."

"No kidding!" Tamar's smile widened as more girls clustered around her. "Too bad I didn't see it myself. Not much of a welcome if I don't see it, is there?"

Several of them giggled, and Tamar winked at them. "Okay. So how do you know which one I am?"

Another girl spoke up. "You're not Rivka Pollack, 'cause she's in choir. She had a solo with her name on the program."

"So she did, Sherlock Holmes." Tamar was definitely enjoying herself. "Okay, go on."

"You're not Elisheva Conrad," the first girl continued. "She's South African."

"And I'm not?"

"Nope." Another girl, this one with tight black curls, shook her head and grinned. "You're way too American to be South African."

"That's one way of putting it, I suppose." Tamar grinned at the group of girls — fifth graders, she'd already decided — clustering around her. "So what does that leave you with?"

"You're not Rochel Kaplan." The girl with braids sounded decisive. "She's a New Yorker. You don't have a New York accent."

"I should hope not!" Tamar gave a mock shudder. "Me, a New Yorker?"

"So you're either Batsheva Teitelbaum or Tamar Bergman." The girl with tight black curls grinned at her. "You're definitely a Tamar, not a Batsheva!"

"Oh, good. And here I was worried that someone's been calling me the wrong name all along!"

They all laughed. Tamar's eyes glowed. *This* is what she'd had back in Kedzie: younger girls with whom to play and laugh and, at same time, help them mature and grow. What could possibly be better than this?

"Tell you what," she proposed impulsively, looking around at the group of fifth graders. "If the snow stops by then, I'll meet you outside during afternoon recess. We'll have a snowball fight!"

A chorus of excited shouts met her suggestion.

"But we're not allowed outside during recess in this weather," the girl with the black curls protested.

Another girl groaned and nudged her in the ribs. "Oh, come *on*, Chaya Leah!"

Chaya Leah flushed a little. "Well, we're *not*." She turned to Tamar with a faintly pleading look in her eyes. "Can't we get together after school, instead?"

Tamar felt certain that there was some undercurrent of strain lurking just beneath the surface. She didn't understand why, and she felt puzzled and curious by the sudden twang of tension in the air, but she didn't want to destroy the fragile rapport she'd already established with these girls. Now was not the time to push and probe. Her opportunities for that would come later.

"Sure, after school," she said agreeably, looking from one girl to the other. "Why not?"

Chaya Leah's tense shoulders relaxed. "Oh, great!" she exclaimed. She turned to her friends. "After school!"

"Yeah, after school!" The girl with braids whooped and threw the ball high into the air. "Super!"

"Will we have teams, or what?"

"Why not?"

"But not if it's snowing — it's no fun that way." Tamar laughed and chatted with the fifth graders, feeling the old surge of excitement running through her. It was with a distinct feeling of disappointment that she heard the shrill sound of the bell cut through the noisy gym to let them know that recess was over.

"That's that," she said regretfully. "But I'll meet you outside the school on the playground right after school is over!" She winked. "Unless it's still snowing, of course. If it is, we'll have to take a *snow* check."

"We'll be there," they all assured her as they drifted away, heading toward the elementary wing of the school. "Don't worry, we'll be there!"

Tamar watched them go, smiling. Then, remembering exactly which class she had now, she turned away and hurried out of the gym, half-running through the rapidly emptying halls. This was one class she didn't want to miss.

"Elisheva!"

Elisheva Conrad glanced up as Tamar came hurrying up to her locker. "Howzit, Tamar?" she greeted her fellow boarder, a friendly smile lighting her delicate features.

The first time Tamar had heard that South African expression, she hadn't been sure she'd heard correctly. Elisheva always seemed so proper, so correct, that any kind of slang seemed strange coming out of her mouth. By now, however, Tamar simply took it in stride. It was all part of this enigma called Elisheva Conrad: reserved, quiet, finicky, and proper; a mischievous sense of humor, occasional flashes of spunk, an uncommonly firm sense of determination, and a serene resolve.

"Howzit to you, too," she said agreeably. "You ready for class?"

A shadow crossed Elisheva's face. "I hope so," she said, her voice a little distant.

"Want me to help you with that Ramban?" Tamar offered. "I went over it last night, and I'll be glad to go over it with you. It'll just take a second or two."

Elisheva's lips tightened. Not this again! "No, thank you," she said politely but coolly.

Tamar looked a little hurt, but she shrugged it off. "Okay, Elisheva, whatever you want." She flashed her a smile and hurried off toward the classroom, the implied insult already forgotten.

Elisheva followed more slowly, clutching her Chumash notebook in her hand. She wished it wasn't so painfully obvious that she had such a weak background. As it was, Tamar was constantly offering to tutor, to teach, seemingly unaware that her overwhelming enthusiasm only served to make Elisheva more reluctant. While she appreciated Tamar's willingness to help, she wished she wasn't so pushy about it! Why hadn't she gotten the hint yet? Why couldn't she understand that Elisheva didn't want to be patronized, tutored…pitied?

Elisheva sighed. She'd always treasured privacy, the ability to close off the noisy, tumultuous world and lose herself in her own thoughts and dreams, more than anything else in the world. It was her way of making peace with herself, of establishing a sense of balance. But now that she was here in Bloomfield, that option was closed to her. Sharing a basement room together with boisterous Tamar and enigmatic Rochel, Elisheva had been forced to learn how to create her own privacy in the midst of intrusive noise and babble.

Elisheva walked into the ninth-grade classroom and seated herself, ignoring the animated chatter going on around her. Shani, her hostess, was excitedly talking to Bayla Rosner and Suri Nadel, with Tamar and several others animatedly joining the conversation. Elisheva opened her Chumash and turned to the right page, staring somewhat pensively at the closely typeset columns of the Ramban. Maybe she should have taken Tamar's offer after all…?

No! Elisheva sat up straighter. She was no pitiful waif! She had her talents, and she'd make her own place here…no matter how long it took. No matter how hard it would be.

She hoped.

Three

Deep silence, except for the nervous sound of pens scratching on paper. Elisheva toyed nervously with a stray wisp of honey-blond hair, her forehead furrowed and her upper lip caught in her teeth. Her eyes darted from the open Chumash in front of her to the imposing man leaning casually against the teacher's desk at the front of the room.

"*Ein haShechinah shorah al hanevi'im ela bishvil Yisrael.*" Rabbi Levi's sharp brown eyes scanned the sea of intent faces, settling on a girl sitting next to Raizy Segal. "Chedva, would you please give us a brief explanation of what that means and how Rashi relates it to this *pasuk*?"

Elisheva marveled. An entire class discussion spent on a *pasuk* that simply said, "*Vayedaber Hashem el Moshe leimor*"! Who would have imagined it?

Chedva Ellis gulped, then straightened a little in her chair. "Well, it connects to the *pasuk* before, which says '*ka'asher tamu*,' when all the people who were supposed to die in the *midbar* because of *cheit hameraglim* had already died. Only then did Hashem speak to Moshe with '*vayedaber*,' which is a *lashon chibbah*, an expression of love. Rashi says the whole time they were in the *midbar* and the people were dying, one year at a time, Hashem didn't use *lashon chibbah*. That teaches us that when Hashem speaks to a *navi*, it's only for the sake of Yisrael."

"Correct, Chedva. Well said. " Rabbi Levi, the elementary-school principal, stroked at his black beard, a small smile tugging at the corners of his mouth. "Does anyone have any questions about that?" The smile grew a little as he waited for a response.

Elisheva swallowed and stared into her Chumash Devarim. They were learning *parashas Devarim, perek beis*. Her sense of fascinated interest in the subject was overlaid by a sense of dread, of almost desperate nervousness. With her limited background — after all, she and her family had become religious only a few years before — she sometimes felt as if she was drowning in a welter of new impressions and difficult *mefarshim*.

But at the same time, this tall, imposing teacher, whom the Bloomfield girls had spoken about at first in soft tones of awed trepidation, somehow drove her to want to learn, to do the best she possibly could — and a little bit more than that, as well.

It was such a *different* kind of class. Unlike their regular Chumash class, where they were well into their third *sedrah* of the year, Rabbi Levi's Chumash class was still holding in the middle of their second *perek*. They lingered over each *pasuk*, discussing various aspects and absorbing the profound *hashkafah* that could be derived from Moshe Rabbeinu's *mussar* to Bnei Yisrael.

More than anything else, though, Rabbi Levi demanded that they *think*. It wasn't enough just to memorize a translation, parrot an explanation. Like right now, for example. They'd already explained the Rashi, but Rabbi Levi was waiting for someone to come up with a question, an argument. And he wasn't going to give it to them, either. He was going to wait and make them figure out the question themselves.

Elisheva scanned the page. She couldn't read the Rashi very well — she still had trouble with the letters — but as far as she could tell, the whole thing seemed rather straightforward. What could she possibly ask about?

The silence stretched out, growing thinner and thinner until it reached the breaking point, like a thread on the verge of snapping in two. Elisheva looked around the room somewhat desperately. Some girls stared at the ceiling for inspiration, while others bent over their Chumashim, trying to find an answer — or at least a question — in one of the other *mefarshim*. Elisheva looked back down at her own Chumash. Slowly, very slowly, she was beginning to learn which *mefareish* to look at for which topic — *Sifsei Chachamim* for explanations on Rashi, for example, and Ibn Ezra for explanations on *dikduk*. But while she was learning where to look, she still didn't know how to understand.

"All right." A soundless sigh of relief rustled through the room as Rabbi Levi broke the silence. "I'll help you girls along with it. '*Ko somar l'Bais Yaakov...*' "

Tamar started, her face lighting up with sudden understanding, and she shot her hand up in the air. Rabbi Levi nodded and smiled at her. "Yes, Tamar?"

"Hashem spoke to the women with the *lashon* of '*vayomer*' and to the men with the *lashon* of '*vayedaber*,' because the women only needed the softer *lashon* of saying and not speaking."

"That's right." Rabbi Levi nodded. "You're on the right track. Can you tell me how that applies?"

Elisheva's shoulders sagged. All that information seemed to be at everyone's fingertips — everyone's but hers. She didn't even know what they were talking about. She'd never heard of the *pasuk* that Rabbi Levi quoted. How would she ever be able to participate fully? It was so frustrating sometimes. Wasn't there any way she could take her knowledge, the skills she already had, and apply them as well?

Tamar was continuing, carefully feeling her way through her question, pleased that she had the opportunity to speak up in this very fascinating class. "Well… if '*vayedaber*' is the harsher *lashon*, why is it called *lashon chibbah*? Wouldn't a softer *lashon* be called an expression of love?"

"Excellent." Rabbi Levi steepled his fingers, his intent gaze sweeping the sea of rapt faces. "We have what appears to be a contradiction. Surely we do not shout and scream at someone we love. We speak softly, gently. Would anyone care to venture an answer? The Kli Yakar answers the question for us."

The Kli Yakar? Elisheva squinted at her Chumash, finally locating the *peirush* on the left-hand side of the page. Why, it was over ten lines long! How could she ever figure it out?

A soft exclamation of pleased understanding escaped Raizy Segal, and she raised her hand excitedly.

"Yes, Raizy?"

"*Lashon* '*medaber*' is *mussar*, and giving *mussar* is love!"

"Exactly." Rabbi Levi straightened and began to pace the front of the room, turning his head to stare at his students with dark-eyed intensity. "Think about it, girls. A child runs carelessly into the street. His mother catches him and gives him a good spanking. Such a horrible mother, spanking her child! How could she do such a thing?" His eyebrows arched, and a soft rustle of amusement ran through the room as his deep voice became a high-pitched whine. Then, in his regular voice, Rabbi Levi added quietly, "I wouldn't think very much of a mother who did not administer that spanking. It's her love for her son that leads her to do it, to teach him that what he did was wrong and dangerous. Admonishing a person, giving him *tochachah*, is love, because it shows that we want him to improve. We care about his improvement. If we didn't care, we wouldn't bother to give *mussar*."

Rabbi Levi paced back toward the desk, letting his words sink in. Nobody said a word.

"Would somebody care to give an example?" he invited after a moment. He glanced around the room at the few hands raised in the air. "Shoshanah?"

"David HaMelech didn't give *mussar* to Avshalom, and Avshalom eventually rebelled against him."

"Very good, Shoshanah. You're not doing somebody a favor if you don't give them *mussar*. '*Hochei'ach tochi'ach es amisecha.*'" Elisheva obediently copied the phrase into her notebook, grateful to Rabbi Levi for writing it on the board so she could spell it properly.

"Look at the Kli Yakar, please. He gives another

example — something we have already learned this year."

Heads bent feverishly over Chumashim. Elisheva squinted at the closely printed lines, wishing she could understand. All those abbreviations just made things worse…

Hands shot up all over the room. Elisheva glanced up, then bit her lip and stared fiercely at her Chumash. Why couldn't she understand? Why?

"Yes, Bayla?"

"The Chumash says '*Eleh hadevarim*' when Moshe Rabbeinu began speaking. That's also *lashon vayedaber*, and he's giving *mussar*."

"Very good. Rochel, will you read the Kli Yakar for us, please?"

Rochel's clipped New York drawl sounded clearly in the hushed room as she read through the *peirush*. Elisheva fought down a sharp pang of envy. How could she read so easily? How did she know where to pause, where to stop and translate, how to read all those confusing abbreviations?

"That last point is important," Rabbi Levi stressed as Rochel finished reading. "If *mussar* is not given in a strong fashion, it's not going to sink in. For example, if a teacher administers an extra homework assignment as a punishment, she is certainly not doing it for enjoyment. After all, that's just another thirty papers she will have to correct. Why bother? Why not just tell her students that they were misbehaving, and leave it at that?" He stopped and turned, pointing a finger with alarming suddenness at Elisheva. "Elisheva? What do you think?"

Elisheva gulped, sat up a little straighter, and tried to put her thoughts into words. If she couldn't read a Rashi yet, at least she could participate in class discussions. She felt a sudden surge of gratitude to Rabbi Levi for letting her speak up when she was able to do so.

"Well…Rabbi Levi said that *mussar* has to be given in a strong way for it to really be felt. A student might not remember being yelled at, but she'll certainly remember having to lose half an hour of her free time when she gets home from school."

"Exactly." Elisheva felt her cheeks grow warm at Rabbi Levi's smile of approval. "Harsh words are often a sign of love. And here, Hashem did not speak in *lashon chibbah* to Moshe Rabbeinu. Moshe, who ascended to *shamayim* to receive the Torah. Moshe, who spoke to Hashem face to face. Moshe, the foremost leader of Klal Yisrael. Why? Because even Moshe, great as he was, received his *nevuah* for the sake of Bnei Yisrael."

Rabbi Levi paused for a moment, then continued in a softer voice. "It is Klal Yisrael as a whole that is truly important. We, each of us, join together to create a whole being — Klal Yisrael — that is infinitely greater than the sum of its parts. And we must realize that it is our responsibility to do what we can, not for ourselves, but for our nation, together."

The bell rang. Nobody moved, or breathed, or even glanced at the clock.

"Moshe Rabbeinu himself represented the *klal*. His entire life was dedicated to serving his nation. His *nevuah*, too, was a service to his nation — for when Bnei Yisrael were in disgrace, so to speak, Moshe Rabbeinu did not receive his *nevuah* with *lashon chibbah*. And what exactly is that *lashon chibbah*? *Mussar*. To care enough about somebody that you want to help them to improve, to learn, to do better."

Tamar's eyes shone. Yes. This was her entire being: to help others.

Rabbi Levi paused again, allowing the message to penetrate, then smiled and said in his normal tone, "Please prepare through *pasuk chaf gimmel* for tomorrow with Rashi and Seforno. In addition, please look up the references Rashi brings down in *chaf gimmel* so that the explanation is clear. I would like to be able to discuss Hashem's *hashgachah pratis* tomorrow — how the intricacies and twists of history are always for a purpose, even if that purpose is decades, or even centuries, in the future." He closed his Chumash and kissed it. "You're dismissed, girls."

Notebooks closed. Chumashim were put away. They stood respectfully as Rabbi Levi walked out of the room, and several girls followed him out into the hall to ask some questions. As usual, Rabbi Levi listened patiently and with interest, giving each girl a chance to say her piece before answering and explaining.

Elisheva shook her head slowly, a pensive look coming into her light blue eyes. She could understand why the entire elementary student body was more than a little scared of the tall principal. But the entire ninth-grade class had rapidly come to realize that Rabbi Levi's Chumash class, with its emphasis on *hashkafah*, was a fascinating challenge. True, Rabbi Levi expected, and demanded, a lot from his high school students; but he also made it clear that he was confident that they were capable of meeting those high standards. Nobody, but nobody, wanted to disappoint him by doing anything less than her best.

The class was so inspiring. She just wished there was some way she could participate more, understand more easily. It was just a matter of time, she supposed, before that would happen. At least she hoped so. Just a matter of time…

"That was such a great class!" Tamar zoomed over to Elisheva's desk, grinning. "I've never had such an inspiring teacher in my life. Don't you wish you could —"

"Elisheva, did you hear what's up?" Chana Hochberg came striding toward her and placed her hands, palms down, on Elisheva's desk, leaning forward with a sparkle of excitement in her eyes. "We went to Rebbetzin Falovitz at recess time, and we got permission to make a band choir!"

"A band choir?" Elisheva repeated, puzzled. "What's a band choir?"

"That sounds neat," Tamar interjected happily. "Elisheva, you'll really have a chance to shine!"

"But what's a band choir?"

"We'll only have five or six girls singing. The main thing will be the music."

"It's great, Elisheva!" Tamar was full of enthusiasm for everything, as usual. But this time, Elisheva couldn't fault her. She herself felt a surge of pleasure, of excitement, at the thought of a performance where she could really play well.

"Sure. That sounds wonderful." She smiled up at the band leader. "When would we have it?"

"But there's more." Chana didn't even seem to hear Elisheva's question. Her voice was charged with a tremor of — what? "The Rebbetzin suggested we have another get-together with a school — maybe Normansville again, or Rollenton. She said she would make some phone calls. Maybe we'll even end up going *there*! Wouldn't that be great?"

Elisheva nodded happily, lost in a world of dreams where musical notes floated on a fluffy cloud and the sweet strains of the flute soared high into the sky. The feelings of discomfort prompted by Tamar's words of praise and admiration for a class she could barely comprehend, the subtle loneliness of being a kind of pariah among her knowledgeable classmates, faded far into the background. Perhaps she couldn't make her mark with classwork, but she had confidence that she could do well in any situation that called for her music.

Surely, that was better than nothing… wasn't it?

Four

The wind announced itself with a howl as Shani pushed her front door open, snowflakes chasing each other into the hallway in their eagerness to invade the Baums' domain. Four bundled-up girls stumbled indoors, hurriedly closing the door behind them. The shriek of the wind cut off abruptly as the door swung shut.

"What a relief!" gasped Tamar, pulling her scarf off and shaking snowflakes and wet droplets off her thick hair. "Too bad, though. I'd planned to have a snowball fight if it would've stopped snowing. If it's this bad in December, what's it going to be like in February?"

"You mean it gets *worse*?" Elisheva looked at her, appalled. Bundled up in scarves, sweaters, gloves, earmuffs, and winter jacket, Elisheva still found the fierce, aching cold to be incredible. Used to South African winters, the harsh snows of upstate New York had caught her by surprise. She couldn't help thinking wistfully that it was summer in South Africa right now…her brother Baruch was probably taking a lazy swim in their Olympic-size swimming pool, and her parents might be planning a braai in the backyard for dinner that night…

"Not too much worse," Shani assured her with a faint smile. "Don't worry about it too much."

Elisheva cringed inwardly. She knew she was probably being too sensitive; she still felt just a little out of place here in Bloomfield, a round peg in a square hole or a camera slightly out of focus. But was it just her imagination, or was Shani's tone patronizing?

"Hello, girls." Mrs. Baum's voice floated out of the kitchen door. "Come on in and take something hot to drink."

The four girls, finally divested of a multitude of coats, scarves, and sweaters, filed their way into the warm, bright kitchen. The comforting aroma of bubbling stew wafted out of the simmering pot on the stove. As usual, Mrs. Baum had not found the time to change from her formal wear as her husband's dental secretary, and her neat outfit seemed oddly out of place in the homey setting of the kitchen.

"Hi, Mommy."

"Hello, Mrs. Baum."

"Hi, Mrs. Baum."

"Good afternoon, Mrs. Baum." Elisheva flushed even as she said it. She knew she sounded stilted and formal in her speech.

"Good afternoon to you all. Miserable weather, isn't it?" Mrs. Baum favored them with a wry smile as she lifted a steaming kettle off the stove.

"No question." Shani rubbed her arms briskly. "I wish the school's boiler would break or something. I could use a day or two curled up in bed."

"Couldn't we all?" Mrs. Baum poured boiling water into four waiting mugs. "Here you go, girls. Make yourselves tea or whatever else you'd like." As she put the kettle back on the stove, she gestured with her free hand toward an envelope, stamped and postmarked, lying on the counter. "That's for you, Elisheva."

Elisheva's pale face lit up as she hurried to the counter and reached for the envelope. "Thank you, Mrs. Baum."

"You're welcome. Shani, can I leave you to peel six potatoes and dice them into the stew?"

"No problem, Mommy," Shani assured her.

"Thanks, hon." Mrs. Baum turned to go, then stopped suddenly and turned back. "Oh, and Shani, there's laundry in the washing machine. Please put it in the dryer on perma press."

"Sure." Shani started for the basement door.

"Take a hot drink first. Another few minutes won't make a difference." Mrs. Baum started to turn away again, but looked back after two steps. "Oh! I almost forgot. Elisheva, may I speak with you later? After dinner, perhaps?"

Elisheva started. "Sure, Mrs. Baum," she stammered. "Thank you." A quick smile, a wave of the hand, and Mrs. Baum disappeared upstairs.

Elisheva sat down with the others at the kitchen table, absently stirring her sugarless tea as she opened her letter. Excitement at receiving news from home vied with nervousness at Mrs. Baum's request. What could she possibly want to speak to her about?

There's laundry in the washing machine... Oh! I almost forgot...

Was that it? Something to do with laundry and household tasks of that nature? Had she done something horribly wrong without even realizing it?

Elisheva was all too painfully aware that she was hopeless at dealing with such chores. She'd never needed to manage, back home; laundry, vacuuming, dusting, washing dishes — all such tasks were managed, capably and efficiently, by Maggie, the Conrads' maid. Elisheva had never needed to fold a jersey, much less launder her own linen. And now, living in the Baums' home, she found herself compelled to take neatness and cleanliness into her own amateur hands.

The three boarders shared a room in the basement, and it was up to them to keep it in order. But Elisheva didn't know how, Rochel didn't mind clutter as long as things were clean, and Tamar was almost aggressively messy. No wonder, then, that their room looked like a schizophrenic with a triple personality.

There was a painfully neat circle surrounding Elisheva's bed; a neatness created by awkward labor on her part, by taking twice as long to sweep as it took the others, by folding and refolding her clothing until her jerseys had to be ironed all over again, by squaring all papers and lining up all notebooks on her dusted twice-daily shelf. In direct contrast, Tamar's bed, the lower half of the bunk bed, overflowed with un-smoothed sheets, crumpled wads of paper, clean and dirty laundry jumbled together, and notebooks either leaning precariously off her shelf or already tumbled to the floor. And Rochel? Her bed was made, certainly, and her things were clean; but her Walkman and CDs lay scattered all over her blanket, and her folders and books were strewn all over the Ping-Pong table that the girls used as their desk.

Elisheva had grown up in a palatial South African villa. The artificial brightness of a basement room shared with two others, with the washing machine and dryer behind a screen and a Ping-Pong table for a homework table, served as a constant, jarring note to remind her of just how much she had left behind…

"So, what does the letter say?" Elisheva blinked and looked up into Tamar's friendly, inquisitive eyes.

"What?"

"The letter," Tamar repeated, gesturing at the unread letter in Elisheva's hands. "What's going on in your family?"

Elisheva flushed, loath to admit that she'd been so busy worrying that she'd stared at the letter without really seeing it. "Nothing, really. Nothing at all." She lowered her eyes again and scanned the letter, a faint smile crossing her face at the sight of her mother's sprawling, illegible script. No, nothing really at all. Baruch was doing well in school. The weather was nice and hot. Her father's business was doing well. The Montrose orchestra was performing in Johannesburg; Mum, a cellist in the orchestra, would be staying with an Orthodox family instead of in the hotel with the other members. That was nice. Just regular, ordinary news.

Elisheva reread the last few lines of the letter: *Well, doll, I'm glad you're doing so well in Bloomfield. We miss you here, though. It would be nice to have a go at coming in for a visit, or maybe bringing you home for Pesach. Think about it and let me know. Have a jol, doll — Mum.*

Elisheva sighed and folded the letter, slipping it back into the envelope. Her mother had talked about visiting her before — and possibly bringing her home for Chanukah. She knew it was really wistful thinking on her mother's part. The trouble was, it made for wistful thinking on her part, too…

The rest of that afternoon passed quietly. Shani came down with the three girls to the basement to take care of the laundry, then vanished upstairs to her own room. Rochel, Elisheva, and Tamar sat around the Ping-Pong table, absorbed in their homework. Elisheva found most secular classes to be well within her scope, but she still struggled with her *limudei kodesh*, sitting hunched over her Chumash as she prepared the *pesukim* for tomorrow's class. She always did her Hebrew homework first, saving her English subjects for later. Geometry and home economics were paltry compared to the frustrating complexities of Chumash and Navi.

Tamar, on the other hand, raced through her *limudei kodesh* homework with no trouble at all. It seemed to take her only one tenth of the time it took Elisheva. Even as Elisheva looked wistfully at her fellow boarder, Tamar, humming softly to herself, closed her own Chumash, leaned back precariously in her chair, and pushed it into place on her shelf. She brought the chair down with a loud thump and shoved it back from the table. "Time for a break," she announced. She stretched theatrically and made her way upstairs, taking the steps two at a time. Elisheva heard her greet one of the Baum kids in the kitchen.

Rochel didn't seem to notice she was gone. As usual, she did her homework with the musical privacy of her Walkman, headphones jammed over her ears and shutting out the rest of the world. Foot tapping absently, she labored over a complicated geometry proof. She, too, had already finished her *limudei kodesh* homework. Like Tamar, she had an extensive background that made it so much simpler for her to follow their Hebrew classes.

Elisheva's expression firmed. Enough of this pitying herself! She'd just have to do the best she could, that's all. And if she had to work twice as hard as everyone else, that was just part of the challenge. Practice made perfect, didn't it? The hours and hours she'd spent polishing her music offered ample proof of that. And what worked with the flute would surely work with her lessons; all it would take would be a healthy dose of determination and a lot of good, old-fashioned hard work.

Of course, hard work is never very much fun. But she'd just have to make the best of it…wouldn't she?

"I don't *like* mashed potatoes." Little Estie Baum folded her arms and looked defiant.

"Eat them anyway," Mrs. Baum told her pleasantly as she served her five-year-old daughter a generous helping.

Tamar grinned. More than anything else, supper-time at the Baums' house made her feel right at home. The chatter, the coziness of being gathered around the table together with a family, even the whining and arguing — she could practically close her eyes and picture herself back in Kedzie, with little Avi speaking in his engaging lisp and Yael's sarcastic comments spicing up the dinnertime conversations.

"Any special news today?" Dr. Baum inquired of the table at large.

Mendy waved his fork excitedly. "We got our *mishnayos* tests back today, Daddy. I got a ninety-two."

"Good work!" Dr. Baum beamed.

"Chaim Stefansky's bar mitzvah is coming up next week," twelve-year-old Yitzy volunteered.

"And how many months — days — hours — till yours?" Tamar asked with an impish grin.

"We learned *kamatz*," Estie announced.

Shani leaned forward. "We're making a band choir. Elisheva's going to be the star of the show!"

Every eye turned to look at Elisheva. A flush crept over her delicate features, and she stared fixedly at her plate.

"How nice!" Mrs. Baum exclaimed. Her blue eyes, so much darker than Shani's, shone sapphire-bright. "I hope you'll still be interested in my little suggestion."

"I beg your pardon?" Elisheva looked at her, feeling somewhat confused.

"I'll explain later." Mrs. Baum poured herself a glass of orange juice. "Right after dinner."

Elisheva puzzled over Mrs. Baum's remark. Could it have anything to do with her request earlier in the day? She contributed little to the dinnertime conversation, too busy wondering — and worrying.

Half an hour later, Mrs. Baum seated Elisheva on the couch in the living room and settled down next to her.

"Do you know what P'tach is, Elisheva?"

"I'm afraid not," Elisheva said softly.

"It's a national program in religious schools for helping children with learning disabilities," Mrs. Baum explained. "A branch opened here in Bais Yaakov only a few weeks ago."

Elisheva blanched. Mrs. Baum couldn't mean — she couldn't —

"We're having a parlor meeting next week," Mrs. Baum continued, oblivious to Elisheva's apprehension. "And I was wondering — hoping, really — that you'd be able to help us."

"To help you?" Elisheva repeated, her initial alarm fading somewhat.

"Yes." Mrs. Baum smiled at her warmly. "You know, Elisheva, you're a very talented flautist. Hearing such high-quality music every night — well, it's really something special. It adds such a special tone to our home."

"Thank you," Elisheva managed, blushing furiously.

"I was hoping I would be able to persuade you to come and play for us at the parlor meeting. It would really add the perfect, elegant touch to the evening." Mrs. Baum leaned forward, her face alight with anticipation. "You certainly don't have to, Elisheva, but I really hope you will."

"P-play at your parlor meeting?" Elisheva stammered, her mind a furious whirl of bewilderment and delight. "I-I'd love to! I'd be honored to play."

"Wonderful!" The deep blue eyes shone brightly. "I'll go call Leah now and tell her." Mrs. Baum rose gracefully and smiled down at her boarder. "Thank you so much, Elisheva. It's so kind of you to give us your time like this."

"My pleasure," Elisheva breathed, standing too. Almost in a daze, she moved out of the living room and into the kitchen, heading downstairs.

"What's with you?" Tamar asked her curiously as the South African girl floated down the steps, her eyes dreamy and her face glowing.

Elisheva came abruptly back to earth. She smiled a little sheepishly at Tamar and at Rochel, who was sitting up on her bunk bed, inquisitiveness stamped all over her face.

"Mrs. Baum asked me to play for the P'tach parlor meeting next week," she told the others shyly.

Tamar whooped and bounced off her bed. "Super, Elisheva!"

"Very nice, Elisheva," Rochel agreed, smiling. "Let someone else listen to your classical music for a change."

Elisheva smiled faintly, unsure as ever whether or not she should take Rochel's comments at face value. She crossed the room to her shelf, where she kept her treasured flute neatly stored in its black box.

"What will you play for them?" Tamar asked, coming over to stand next to her.

"I don't know," Elisheva confessed. She picked up one of her dozen music books and flipped aimlessly through the pages. "Maybe Vivaldi...perhaps some Mozart..."

Rochel leaned over the edge of her bed, squinting down at the others. "I'm sure it'll be nice, Elisheva. Whatever you play." For once, her voice was devoid of its usual sarcasm.

"Thank you," Elisheva answered, smiling.

"You'll be great." Tamar slung an overly familiar arm over Elisheva's shoulders. "You can do it, kiddo. No question about it!"

Elisheva winced and moved away as politely as she could, feeling slightly repelled by Tamar's intrusiveness even as she felt her cheeks warm at the compliment.

Her mind flashed back to her thoughts right after Rabbi Levi's class, when she had realized just how long she had to go before she would be able to truly participate in a *limudei kodesh* class.

Perhaps she couldn't make her mark with classwork, but she had confidence that she could do well in any situation that called for her music.

And she would!

Five

The sky was an icy blue, with thin gray clouds scudding across the horizon. The snowstorm had finally blown over, freeing the student body from the confines of the gym. With the shrill jangle of the recess bell, the girls bundled up in coats and scarves and came streaming outdoors, eager for a chance to breathe the fresh, chilly air. The playground of Bais Yaakov of Bloomfield echoed with strangely muffled shouts, as if the snow lying thickly on the ground muted all sounds.

In one corner of the playground, snowballs whizzed thickly through the air, and squeals, whoops, and giggles rang a shrill counterpoint to the thumps as the snowballs landed, more often than not, on target. They'd been planning the snowball fight ever since that first day of the snowstorm, and they threw themselves into it with abandon.

Tamar Bergman's cheeks glowed red from the cold — and the excitement. Surrounded by laughing, shouting fifth graders, she dazzled her fellow teammates with her unerring aim, sending snowballs flying across the empty space between the forts to land squarely on an opponent's nose, hair, or mouth. At the same time, she simply managed to be elsewhere any time a snowball came sailing in her direction. Her teammates cheered wildly every time she scored a hit.

"All right, Tamar!" shouted Chaya Leah, the girl with the tight black curls. Jumping up and down with excitement, she wound up and threw a snowball at the opposition. The snowball sailed gracefully through the air and landed just a few inches shy of the fort. The girl gave a mock groan. "How do you manage to throw it so far?" she demanded of the ninth grader.

Tamar looked down at her and grinned. "Practice, Chaya Leah," she chuckled. "Like this." She reared back and hurled a chunk of snow across to the other team, hitting the girl with the braids squarely in the face.

Chaya Leah laughed and waved at her friend, who was spluttering and clawing at the snow. "Too bad, Shosh!" she yelled. "Better luck next time!"

Shosh, who had finally managed to claw the snow from her face, yelled back, "I'll get you for this, Chaya Leah! You just watch!"

At that moment, the bell rang. Chaya Leah groaned and got up. "Oh, well," she sighed. "Recess is over. I guess we'd better —" She stopped short as a well-aimed snowball hurtled through the chilly air and landed in her open mouth. Startled, she took a staggering step backwards and sat down hard.

Tamar burst out laughing and leaned down to help the fifth grader to her feet. "Better luck next time," she teased, her voice mimicking Chaya Leah's own.

Chaya Leah, still coughing snow, grinned and took the proffered hand, using it to haul herself up. "You're all right, Tamar Bergman," she declared.

At that moment, wet and snowy as she was, Tamar wouldn't have changed places with anybody else in the world.

"After *bnei Eisav* rejected the Torah, Hashem offered it to the children of Yishmael. What happened?" Rabbi Levi's sharp gaze roved the room. "Shula?"

Shula Goldman straightened in her chair. "*Bnei Yishmael* asked Hashem what was in the Torah, and Hashem told them that it said they couldn't steal. *Bnei Yishmael* said that, in that case, they weren't interested."

"Correct. Tell me, Elisheva — don't you think Hashem *knew* what they were going to say?"

"Of course," Elisheva said quickly. "But — but Rashi says that Hashem wanted to give them a chance first, even though He knew what the answer would be."

"That's right. Shani, how does that apply to '*midbar Kedeimos*'?"

"Well, Moshe says he learned from Hashem — Who gave the Torah, which came *before* the world, in the *desert* — that he should offer peace to Sichon, even though he knew Sichon would refuse and come out to fight."

"Correct. And what other explanation are we given? Bayla?"

"Moshe learned from Hashem, Who was *before* everything, when Hashem sent him from the *desert* to talk to Pharaoh, even though Hashem could have just zapped Mitzrayim with a lightning bolt instead of giving the country so many chances."

"Very good, Bayla." Rabbi Levi smiled at them. "I'm pleased to see that you girls have learned how to read a *peirush* and apply it. Therefore, I believe you are ready for your first major assignment."

A wave of uneasiness rippled through the room. A major assignment?

"I would like you to choose a topic from Chumash — any topic that interests you — and explain it thoroughly, as if you were teaching it yourself." The corner of Rabbi Levi's mouth tipped up in a sardonic smile. "Believe me, girls, you must know a topic very, very well before you can teach it to others. I will expect you to give me your topic this week. This project will be due five weeks from now — say, the Wednesday of the second week of Shevat. We will devote class time to questions once a week, so I will have the opportunity to help you with any difficulties." He paused. "Any questions?"

Only their respect for their teacher and former principal kept the girls from exclaiming and discussing the issue. Such a difficult assignment! How would they manage?

Chaya rose her hand a little timidly. "Can — can we get help on this?"

"Of course," Rabbi Levi said pleasantly. "As long as you get *help*, not dictation. I am not interested in a paper written by your fathers or older brothers or anyone else. I am interested in a paper written by you. Is that clear?"

It was, without a doubt.

"Furthermore," Rabbi Levi went on, "I know your styles of writing well enough to recognize anything that would be out of context. I would be *extremely* disappointed to find any copying or evasions. For example, if I find half a page that is a direct quote from an English translation of the Ramban..." He did not finish the sentence. The intent look in his dark eyes said it for him.

Elisheva swallowed hard. Help! How would she ever be able to complete such an assignment?

"For tomorrow, please prepare up to *shishi*. You're dismissed, girls. Have a good day."

The girls jumped to their feet out of respect for their teacher. Elisheva closed her Chumash and stared at her notebook without really seeing it. It was going to be hard, so very hard; but she'd manage. Somehow. She *wanted* to be able to manage. Rabbi Levi thought she could do it; wasn't it possible that he was right?

"Elisheva, aren't you coming to lunch?" Frumi Scharf, the high school dance head, leaned over Elisheva's desk. "C'mon, I'm starved."

"Coming," Elisheva said absently. She stood up, and almost collided with an exuberant Tamar.

"What an assignment!" Tamar gushed, her dark eyes sparkling with excitement. "I'm gonna work really hard on it. This is going to be super great!"

Elisheva smiled faintly at her, then gathered up her books and made her way toward the door.

"Elisheva?" The South African girl turned around quickly. Rabbi Levi came walking toward her, an intent but kind expression on his face.

"Y-yes, Rabbi Levi?" she gulped.

"I just wanted to tell you that I have every confidence in you. I am sure you'll be able to do a good job on this assignment. If you need any assistance, I'll be glad to work with you during lunchtime or recess."

"Thank you," she breathed, feeling a sudden surge of gratitude that this tall, imposing principal was such an understanding teacher.

"You're welcome." Rabbi Levi nodded briskly at her and the others and walked away.

Rochel Kaplan lay on her back on her upper bunk, headphones jammed over her ears. The CD had ended several minutes ago, but she didn't move to turn it over. She wasn't in the mood for music; and she wasn't in the mood for talking, either. Besides, Elisheva was practicing her flute again, determined to be note-perfect for her performance the following night — she'd prefer not to have to listen to the same tune for the fortieth time. And Tamar was upstairs, keeping an eye on the kids for Mrs. Baum, who had gone to a meeting somewhere together with Shani. It was better this way; let Elisheva think she was listening to her Walkman. She would leave her alone — Elisheva was fiercely defensive about her own and other people's privacy — and it would give her time to think.

For a long time, she'd avoided the issue completely. Her mother hadn't pushed her; she'd given her time to think, to contemplate, to summon up the courage to face the inevitable. The trouble was that Rochel didn't want to face it at all.

She rolled over onto her stomach, punching moodily at her pillow. If only she could just ignore the events happening in New York, as if the Kaplan family was no longer related to her. As if her last name was still Saltzberg. She'd settled nicely into life here in Bloomfield; sometimes, for a moment or two, she could even manage to forget about the aching tragedy that was the very center of her life.

Sometimes.

Her eye lit on the faded maroon siddur perched on the very edge of her shelf. Her father had given her that siddur six years ago in recognition of the stubborn persistence with which she had mastered a difficult school assignment, a persistence that was to become an integral part of her being. The siddur had become, in some peculiar fashion, the physical symbol of her longing for the days when her father was still alive. The letters that had once spelled out her name in bright gold were faded now; the smooth, pristine maroon leather had become scuffed and worn; and her memories of her father, of his warm smile, his easy laugh, his gentle understanding, his beautiful, almost haunting voice — those memories seemed to grow fainter with each passing day, almost in direct proportion to the number of scuff marks on the siddur.

Rochel shivered. She didn't want her memories to fade. She wished there was some way she could talk to her father again for just five minutes, to pour out her fears and her worries and let him soothe her anxieties with his gentle wisdom.

But it couldn't happen. It never would, ever again…

And now? Rochel bit her lip. For the last six weeks, her mother had been asking her, ever so gently, to please come home for a Shabbos. Her lame excuses and evasions no longer served their purpose. Very soon — if not next week, then the one after that — she was going to have to travel to New York and spend a weekend with her mother. And her stepfather. And her stepbrother. And her stepsister…

Dovid actually wasn't that much of a problem. Her stepfather's son was already twenty-three; he was learning in Chicago Telshe, and he only came home for *yamim tovim*. Even when he was in the house, he avoided Rochel as much as she avoided him.

But her stepsister! Rochel grimaced to herself, her fingers curling into fists of their own volition. Leah Malka Kaplan had been attending a second year of seminary in Yerushalayim the year her father had married Rochel's mother. She'd delayed her departure to Eretz Yisrael for the wedding, but Rochel, her sense of outraged betrayal coloring every perception, had studiously ignored her. Right after the *sheva brachos*,

Leah Malka had left — and Rochel had begun a year of fury and frustration, a year of anger and misery and cold, hostile silences. And by the time Leah Malka came back to America after spending her summer with family in England, Rochel had already left to attend school in Bloomfield.

No, the two of them had never really met. And Rochel wasn't so sure she wanted to…

But that choice was not hers to make. Unless, of course, she planned to stay here in Bloomfield until Leah Malka got married. She supposed she couldn't really get away with refusing to attend the wedding.

Rochel couldn't stop her lips from curving up in a sardonic smile. It was all very well for her to visualize Leah Malka's wedding. Unfortunately, her trip home for Shabbos was most likely to happen before that; she sort of doubted that Leah Malka, who wasn't engaged yet, would be getting married sometime in the next week.

Sighing, Rochel rolled over again, gazing up at the ceiling as she pulled the headphones off her ears and tossed the Walkman into the corner of her bed, letting the sweet strains of Elisheva's flute wash over her. She'd just have to cope. Somehow.

After another minute or two, Elisheva lowered her flute with a sense of reluctance. She closed the music book spread out in front of her and began to disassemble the instrument.

"Nice, Elisheva," called Tamar as she bounced down the steps, giving her a thumbs-up.

"Thank you." Elisheva smiled and placed her flute carefully in its black case. "I hope the performance goes well tomorrow…"

"It will," Tamar assured her. "Don't worry." She tossed her notebook onto the homework table. "I got a lot of research done tonight. This assignment is really something. I hope Rabbi Levi likes my topic."

Elisheva felt a twinge of uneasiness. She hadn't even started working on Rabbi Levi's major assignment yet; all her attention had been focused on tomorrow night's performance at the P'tach parlor meeting. She still had another four weeks, though. She shouldn't have any trouble managing — she hoped.

"Mrs. Baum and Shani came home," Tamar was saying. "They both looked pretty strange. I wonder if —"

She stopped at the sound of uneven footsteps coming down the stairs. Moments later, Shani appeared in view, a dazed look on her face.

"Shani?" Rochel turned her head. "What's up?"

"I — you — we —"

Rochel sat up, looking a little alarmed. "Sit down, Shani," she ordered. "Take a deep breath."

Obediently, Shani wobbled over to a chair and sank down into it, taking a deep breath and releasing it slowly. After a moment or two, she looked up, her face a little calmer.

"Sorry," she said, smiling a little sheepishly. "It's just — well, a little overwhelming."

"What is?"

Shani took another deep breath. "Do you remember that writing campaign the elementary started a week or two ago?"

"The one for that kid in Switzerland who was in the car accident?" Tamar asked.

"Uh-huh. Well — you see, the newspaper staff sent her a whole synopsis of the way things are run on the *B.Y. Times*. And Raizy Segal and I sort of dropped in and jotted down a few lines, too. And now — and now —"

"What?" Rochel demanded, feeling a little impatient.

"You're not going to believe this."

"Try us." Rochel folded her arms.

"Mimie's father," Shani said carefully, taking yet another deep breath to calm the rising surge of wild excitement bubbling up inside her, "came to school today."

"Here? In Bloomfield?"

"Yes. He flew in. And he invited all of us — the girls on the staff now, and Raizy and I — to come visit his daughter in Switzerland. For two weeks."

They stared.

Tamar was the first one to recover, although she still felt incredulous. "You mean he's taking you all back to Switzerland with him?"

"Yes." Shani's eyes glowed. "For two weeks! Rabbi Levi and Rebbetzin Falovitz discussed it this afternoon, and they gave their okay. And we had a meeting tonight —"

"That's where you went?"

"Yeah." Shani shook her head, marveling. "Can you imagine it? We're going in three days from now. To Switzerland!"

"Amazing," breathed Elisheva. "What a time you'll have!"

"Some *refuah sheleimah* trip!" Tamar laughed.

"Very nice, Shani," Rochel said quietly. "I'm sure you'll enjoy it."

"Oh, we will," Shani said happily, a delighted laugh escaping her. "I've never even been out of the country before, unless you count a trip to Toronto. Isn't it great? Three days isn't much time, of course, but we'll manage somehow. We have to make sure that we —"

Rochel tuned her out. Sinking back down into a laying position, she deliberately turned her face toward the wall, blinking hard. It was so unfair. Why did she have to face the strain and tension, the conflicts churning through the Kaplan home, while Shani

Baum, happy and content in her little hick town, went flying off to Switzerland on a dream vacation? Why should —

Rochel stopped suddenly, surprised — and a little alarmed — at the intensity of her feelings. She knew she had flaws — many of them, to be sure — but jealousy was not part of her nature. She shouldn't be reacting this way. It was just another symptom, another chink in her defense as she faced up to the inevitable reality of going back to the Kaplan house and facing her step-father.

Rochel chewed on her thumbnail. Maybe it would be better to get it over with, to drive the canker out of her system and put it all behind her.

Maybe.

And maybe not.

Elisheva's bed, usually so neat and spotless, was covered with discarded outfits. Rochel, a look of abstract concentration on her face, combed Elisheva's hair, arranging it in a neat French braid. Tamar surveyed the pile of clothing with a critical eye. Elisheva's outfits were all frilly, starchy, and elegant. Tamar's wardrobe was chosen with an eye toward comfort, not looks.

"I like the blouse with the embroidery on the front, together with the matching skirt."

"Which one?" Elisheva asked, turning to look.

"Don't move," Rochel admonished, gathering up the plait that had slipped out of her hand.

"Sorry." Elisheva faced front. "Which one, Tamar?" she asked again, this time without turning her head.

"That's right," Rochel agreed, her fingers moving smoothly from one honey-blond braid to another. "Which one *do* you mean, Tamar? You've just described half of Elisheva's wardrobe." She deftly tucked a few escaping hairs into place.

"This one." Tamar held up a floral skirt in blues and greens with a faint hint of red.

Rochel looked up for a moment, her hands still absorbed in their task. "That's a nice one," she approved. "Wear that, Elisheva." She obligingly turned Elisheva's head for her so she could look.

Elisheva frowned, her forehead puckering with indecision. "Are you sure?"

"You can wear this one, instead," Tamar offered, dropping the first skirt and holding up another one. "Or this one — or this one — or this one." She gave Elisheva an impish grin.

Footsteps sounded on the stairs, and Shani came into view. "How are we doing?" she asked, a current of excitement rippling through her voice.

"Just fine," Rochel replied without looking up from the last few strands. "We've taken care of Elisheva's hair, but we haven't decided what she's wearing yet."

Elisheva rolled her eyes. "You'd think Elisheva would be capable of deciding things for herself!"

"Oh, no, Elisheva," Tamar said, her face straight. "She can't."

Elisheva gave a little half-laugh. Shani, also chuckling, came across the room. "We want you to look just right, Elisheva. After all, you're representing us all."

A shadow crossed Elisheva's delicate features. "Yes…"

"Hey!" Rochel tapped her sharply on the shoulder. "No worrying allowed."

"Sure." Elisheva managed a weak smile. "No worrying allowed."

"What time are we supposed to be there?" Tamar demanded.

"Eight thirty," Rochel answered impatiently. "I've told you that twice already."

"That gives us only half an hour. Will we be ready in time?"

"I'll be ready." Rochel shrugged eloquently. "The question is, will *you* be ready?"

"Oh, sure, no problem at all. I just have to grab an outfit —" Tamar gave a free demonstration by darting over to the clothes bar, grabbing the sleeve of her favorite lavender dress, and yanking hard, wrenching it off the hanger and sending the hanger flying halfway across the room in the process. "— and put it on. See? Nothing to it."

Elisheva winced. "I'm afraid it will take me a little longer than that," she said somewhat tartly. "Are you finished yet, Rochel?"

"Yup, all done — except for the bow." Rochel tightened the ponytail holder at the bottom. "That'll have to wait until you get dressed, so we know what clip will match."

"Thank you." Elisheva rose from her chair and turned to smile at Rochel. "I appreciate it."

"All part of the service, ma'am," Rochel drawled, grinning back.

"Well, I'm going upstairs to change." Shani headed back toward the steps. "I'll be back soon."

Time seemed to quicken as the girls raced against the clock to get ready to accompany Elisheva, budding musical star of Bloomfield, to the Chinns' house for her debut performance. Elisheva, who had finally chosen the floral print skirt that Tamar had recommended in the first place, had to consciously stop her hands from trembling as she buttoned her blouse. A quick tug here, a small adjustment there, and she was ready — she hoped.

"My mother's going to warm up the car," Shani yelled down the stairs. "Are you coming?"

"Yes," Tamar yelled back. She gave her hair one more casual swipe before hurrying up the stairs. Rochel, however, stayed back and waited for Elisheva to pick up her flute case and the collapsible music stand.

"Are you ready?" she asked quietly.

Elisheva, her face pale, licked her lips before replying. "I think so," she said softly. "Yes."

"Then let's get going, Milady. Your chariot awaits you."

Smiling faintly, Elisheva made her way upstairs, with Rochel right behind her. They met Shani and Tamar in the front hall, busy struggling into winter coats.

"Let's get going," Shani urged, her tone impatient. "My mother's waiting."

Elisheva didn't say a word as the four girls went out into the cold night. She'd practiced her piece so often that she could close her eyes and visualize the sheet music. She practically heard the notes echoing through her dreams; but she still quaked with apprehension. She'd never played solo before. Would she do as well as she hoped to — as she *wanted* to? This was her one greatest talent. Oh, she was part of the dance group, but it wasn't the same. It was music that had always been an integral part of her. If she failed here tonight in this, her first opportunity to really demonstrate her abilities in the soaring, pristine realm of music, how would she ever be able to hold up her head again?

The windshield wipers blurred against the glass, fighting the gusty swirls of snowflakes whirling down against the blackness of the night. Elisheva swallowed hard against the queasiness creeping through her as the Baums' minivan turned onto the Chinns' street. Both sides of the road were lined with closely parked cars; there was nowhere for Mrs. Baum to park. Elisheva's lip quivered. The parlor meeting must have full attendance. All those ladies, gathered together and watching and listening to her…

"Let me drop you off here, girls," Mrs. Baum suggested, braking in front of the Chinns' home. The driveway and sidewalk were cleared of snow, opaque crystals of salt glinting in the reflected gleam of the car's headlights. "I'll park around the corner and walk back."

"Sure," Elisheva gulped.

"I'll come with you, Mommy," Shani offered.

The three out-of-towners got out of the car and made their way up the front walk. The front door was open, a golden circle of welcoming light against the chill darkness.

Elisheva suddenly stopped. She could not advance against the dreadful nervousness, against the terror of facing the ultimate horror of failure. "I can't," she whispered; not to Tamar, not to Rochel. To herself, perhaps. To her mother far away in Montrose, South Africa. To the winter night, to the uncaring stars…

But it was Tamar who answered. "Yes," she said softly, all exuberance suppressed in this moment of caring. "Yes, you can."

And Elisheva, she who supposedly hated to be touched, reached out, groping, to cling tightly to her friends' hands. Together, the three of them paced forward, ready to face the challenge.

Six

Undulating waves of music flowed and rippled through the otherwise silent room. On sofas, chairs, and benches, elegantly dressed women leaned forward, enraptured by the hauntingly sweet strains of Elisheva's flute. Elisheva, oblivious to her intent audience, had eyes only for the sheet of music, all her concentration focused on producing the crystal-clear tones of Mozart's concerto. All thoughts of nervousness had long since faded away. She could have been alone, back in her lovely upstairs bedroom in the Conrads' South African villa, indulging in her nightly half hour of practice.

Shani, Rochel, and Tamar, together with the Chinn twins, leaned against the back wall of the room, faint smiles on their faces as they listened. Elisheva was certainly doing them all proud. Shani couldn't help remembering the fantasy that had sprung out of her resentment when she'd discovered that several Bloomfield girls would be attending school in New York instead of staying home in Bais Yaakov High: a vision of her boarders astounding all and sundry with their brilliant talents, leaving Mashy Bonner and the other "traitors" out in the cold. Surely, her dream was coming true, right before her eyes!

A final arpeggio soared upwards, then faded slowly away. Regretfully, Elisheva lowered her flute, coming back to earth with a thud.

There was a moment of silence. Then, all at once, the spell broke and the room burst into applause.

Elisheva stood there, head bowed slightly, cheeks bright red from pleasure and embarrassment. The ladies clustered around her, talking and cooing and exclaiming, and Elisheva, with her typical dignified poise, answered and explained and smiled.

"Gorgeous," Chinky Chinn breathed.

"Stunning," her sister Pinky agreed.

"Isn't she great?" Shani beamed fondly at her boarder, surrounded by admiring ladies. "She's really something special."

Rochel smiled and nodded, eyes glistening with unshed tears. Music meant more to her than it did to any of the others, and while the flute was hardly similar to the hauntingly lovely *niggunim* her father had composed, she could not help but be moved by beautiful melodies, no matter what form they took.

Only Tamar's smile seemed strained. Tamar Bergman, the rabbi's daughter, so used to being right in the middle of everything, stood by the sidelines, her mouth stretched in a painful grin. Tamar Bergman, of Kedzie, Illinois, the leader, the teacher, the one who had helped so many others, had to turn away, almost in physical pain, from the sight of her fellow boarder basking in a glow of admiration.

Tamar had never actually realized how much it meant to her to be able to do, to help, to achieve. But now, watching Elisheva shine despite her weak background in formal Jewish learning, Tamar felt a bitter, twisted canker growing somewhere within her — a feeling of envy, of anger, of cold misery. Why couldn't she make her mark in Bloomfield? Why couldn't she do what she did so well and help others learn and grow?

Tamar's shoulders suddenly straightened. Her dark eyes flashed, and her teeth set together as she banished the growing pangs of envy. No! She would *not* succumb to jealousy and resentment. She was happy for Elisheva. All this meant was that she, too, needed to do something, to achieve a position for herself. She *could* make her mark here. And she would!

Tamar suited action to words the following after-noon. At recess time, while the other ninth graders gathered in small groups to discuss the future band choir, Tamar made her way to the elementary wing. Here, the chatter and talk was different; the voices were more high-pitched and shrill, the treble babble of their giggles and laughter less self-conscious. She wandered down the hall, past classrooms filled with tiny desks and tinier students, until she reached the fifth-grade classroom.

They were such a good bunch of kids. They'd gotten along so well right from the start, and the snowball fight had shattered any lingering feelings of awkwardness or shyness. She loved them all, every single one, although she only knew a handful of names — Bracha, Chaya Leah, Shosh, Shevi, Tzivia — and no last names at all. But she still loved them, for their bright interest in life that had not yet been soured by growing maturity, for their liveliness and good nature and high spirits. She wanted to get to know them better, to become an in-tegral part of their lives, to teach them and help them and —

A strange, disagreeable buzz reached Tamar's ears, growing louder as she approached the half-closed door of the fifth-grade classroom. It was a sound that seemed oddly out of place in the cheerful atmosphere of recess, a discordant note that jangled on the nerves.

It was the sound of girls shouting, anger coloring their voices with an ugly tinge. Without stopping to think, Tamar yanked open the door and went inside.

The fifth graders were clustered in the back of the room, yelling and reinforcing each other's resentments.

"It's not fair…" Tzivia moaned at the ceiling.

"I can't believe it!"

"He's so mean. How can he do this to us?" Shevi's question was largely rhetorical. "Why can't he just tell us we were wrong and leave it at that?"

"Yeah! How come he has to go cancel a special treat for one little thing?"

On and on, in circular arguments, the girls shouted, complaining at the top of their lungs. All but one. Chaya Leah, her tight black curls somehow drooping, stood as far away from the others as possible, pretending to be absorbed in reading the compositions stapled to the bulletin board. Her face, however, betrayed her; her expression was a study of humiliation, aversion, and distress. The complaints continued.

"That's not fair, we declare, this is it, we quit!" Shosh stamped her foot angrily.

"I can't believe he could be so mean…"

"It wouldn't hurt him to treat us a little nicely…"

"No wonder everybody's scared of him!"

"I was looking forward to it so much…"

"HELLO!"

Silence fell over the room. As one, all the fifth-grade heads turned toward the classroom door, where Tamar stood, hands on her hips.

"Good afternoon to you all," she said pleasantly. "I'm not going to ask how you're doing, because I think I don't want to know. I came to invite you all to a get-together after Bnos this week in the Baums' basement. Refreshments will be served, if you'll trust my baking. Interested?"

Slow, shy smiles appeared on a few faces, like the sun peeking through storm clouds.

"That would be nice," Shosh said softly.

"Yeah," agreed another girl whose name Tamar hadn't learned yet.

Others nodded.

"What would we do?" another girl asked.

"Oh, I'll think of something," Tamar assured them, grinning.

"Sounds good to me," declared Tzivia.

"And me!" announced another.

"Me, too," Chaya Leah said from her vantage point near the bulletin board, her voice barely audible.

The air in the room suddenly turned to ice. Every eye turned to stare at Chaya Leah, and the faces were anything but friendly. Chaya Leah endured it for a few moments, staring back at her fellow classmates, a defiant look in her eye keeping the furies at bay.

Then her resolution crumbled, her face crumpled, and she pushed blindly past Tamar and bolted from the room.

Tamar stared after her for a moment, then turned back to the rest of the girls. She looked directly at Shosh; her previous associations with the fifth graders had taught her that the girl was Chaya Leah's best friend.

"May I ask what that was all about?" she asked as mildly as possible.

Shosh avoided Tamar's gaze, shifting her weight from one foot to another.

"Could it possibly have something to do with the uproar I heard when I came into the room?" Tamar asked the question carefully. She didn't want to appear to lecture them; she didn't want to damage the rapport, still rather fragile, that she had managed to develop with them.

"Well…" Shosh mumbled. "Well…"

Another girl burst out with the answer, the words tumbling over themselves. "We were supposed to go on a field trip, and Rabbi Levi canceled it!"

The uproar started again. "It's not fair… He's so mean… How can he do this… We deserve to go…"

The lights suddenly flicked off. The girls stopped again, shocked, and whirled around to face an exasperated Tamar.

"Am I going to get the story, or what?" she demanded as she turned the lights back on. She pointed a finger at Shevi, who had been slouching against the wall and moping instead of yelling. Maybe she would be a little calmer than the others. "Shevi, what's going on?"

Shevi scowled but answered. "We — well, we did something wrong." She flushed a little. "And we were supposed to go on a field trip tomorrow. Rabbi Levi canceled it." Her words came faster now, almost tumbling over themselves, as if she sought vindication from this ninth grader they all admired. "It's just not fair. We've been looking forward to this for two weeks. And we do one little thing and we can't go. It's not as if we —"

"Hold on a second." Tamar frowned. "What — exactly — does this have to do with Chaya Leah? Why are you all taking this out on her?" She tapped her foot. "Somehow I don't think Chaya Leah made you get in trouble. Right?"

"Of course not," one girl blurted sarcastically. "Chaya Leah never does *anything* wrong."

"Did she tell on you?" Tamar demanded, dreading the answer even as she asked the question. Abandoning a fellow student to her fate, identifying the culprit of some misdeed to the enemy — the teacher — was the one crime for which no child would ever be pardoned. Tamar couldn't imagine that Chaya Leah would do

such a thing, but she couldn't conceive of any other cir-
cumstance that would prompt such a hostile reaction.

"No," Tzivia admitted.

"Then what —"

The end-of-recess bell rang, cutting Tamar off in
mid-sentence. She sighed. "I'd better get going. Try and
cool off a little, huh, guys? I'll see you all, *im yirtzeh
Hashem*, on Shabbos, right after Bnos. Okay?"

"Okay," they murmured back, drifting toward their
seats. Their faces were not exactly happy.

Tamar walked quietly out of the room, her mood
pensive. She'd never expected those kids to react with
such hostility to anything, but she didn't know all the
circumstances. She was a little curious as to exactly
what the class had done wrong, but she wasn't going to
pry; they were obviously pretty ashamed of whatever it
was.

But what she couldn't understand was the treatment they were giving Chaya Leah. Why should they
act as if she were a traitor to the class if she hadn't done
anything wrong? Tamar had already typed Chaya Leah
as being the class goody-goody, but it hadn't seemed to
affect her relationship with her fellow students. As far
as Tamar could tell, they'd merely accepted that Chaya
Leah was unlikely to participate in any kind of prank.
It hadn't made the others despise her. It was just a fact
of life — until recess time today, when they'd faced her

down and treated her like a renegade turncoat, a despicable person who had betrayed them all.

Why? What could possibly cause them to act like that?

As she strode down the hall toward the high school wing, she caught sight of Chaya Leah, slouched near the water fountain, a look of profound gloom written all over her face. Tamar slowed as she neared her, ready to offer any comfort she could.

Then Chaya Leah looked up — past Tamar — and a tentative, uneasy smile crossed her face. Tamar looked curiously over her shoulder, then whirled around, feeling her spine snap straight.

"G-good afternoon, Rabbi Levi," she stammered.

"Good afternoon, Tamar," the imposing principal replied. His expression seemed somewhat distracted. "Aren't you a little late for class?"

"I-I guess so," Tamar said hurriedly. She turned and headed back toward the high school wing, her steps short and fast. But she couldn't help overhearing the conversation between Rabbi Levi and Chaya Leah going on behind her…

"What's wrong, Chaya Leah?"

"Nothing." The sound of scuffling feet reached Tamar clearly.

"Why aren't you in class?" Somehow, the question seemed gentle, almost concerned.

"I'm going back now…" The fifth grader's voice sounded unconvincing.

"Something's troubling you, Chaya Leah. What is it?"

"Nothing, Tatty. Really."

Tatty? Tamar almost fell over with shock. Chaya Leah was Rabbi Levi's *daughter*?

"All right, *zeeskeit*. Go back to class. We'll discuss this at home."

"Okay, Tatty." Slow, dragging footsteps receded into the distance.

Tamar forced herself to keep walking, not daring to look back. Chaya Leah was Rabbi Levi's daughter! She hadn't even known Rabbi Levi had any kids in Bais Yaakov! How could she have been so stupid?

On second thought, however, she couldn't blame herself for not suspecting the truth. She'd never learned any of the fifth graders' last names. It explained so much: Chaya Leah's refusal to participate in any mischief, her classmates' understanding and acceptance of her "goody-goody" behavior, and their anger and resentment today. Unable to protest a punishment which they were reluctant to admit they probably deserved, all their displeasure and hostility had lashed out against Chaya Leah as proxy for her father. No wonder Chaya Leah had looked so miserable. Even if they hadn't treated her in such a fashion, it couldn't have been very pleasant for her to hear her fellow fifth graders complain so vociferously about her father.

Tamar gnawed on her lower lip, mind racing with the possibilities. There had to be something she could do to defuse the situation, to help the fifth graders see they were being unfair to Chaya Leah, to help the young girl regain the trust and friendship of her classmates.

But how?

Seven

Rochel, Elisheva, and Tamar rarely ventured upstairs to Shani's room; Shani usually came down to visit them. On this *motza'ei Shabbos*, however, all three of them were there, Rochel sitting cross-legged on the pale blue carpet, Tamar sprawled in an ungainly fashion on the bed, and Elisheva seated decorously by Shani's desk. Shani rushed back and forth from her closet to her bed, where her suitcase lay open and half-full of clothes.

"What's the weather like in Switzerland, anyway?" Rochel asked.

"Cold, probably," Elisheva remarked. "The Alps, remember?"

"I don't really know," Shani admitted. "But it probably won't be too different from here. It's not like we're going to Yerushalayim!" She chuckled at the thought. "We'd need warmer clothes then. But Switzerland?"

"You're right," Tamar said.

"How do you know?" Rochel demanded.

Tamar smirked at her. "Out-of-towners learn geography, Rochel. Nothing a New Yorker like you would know about."

Elisheva moved quickly to head off another argument of New York vs. Out-of-Town. "What time is the flight tomorrow morning?"

"Early," Shani said a little ruefully. "That's why I want to get packed tonight." She grinned at the threesome. "Not bad, huh? Missing two whole weeks of school!"

"Good thing you're not missing the band choir," Tamar teased.

Shani looked thoughtful. She cast an almost shy glance at Rochel, remembering a conversation the two of them had a few months before. "Maybe," she said slowly, "it'll be good for me not to be around when they're getting things set up."

Rochel winked at her. "Good for you, Shani," she said, her tone emphatic.

"I don't understand," Tamar confessed, looking from Shani to Rochel with a puzzled expression. A quick glance at Elisheva confirmed that the South African girl was equally at a loss to explain what Shani meant.

Shani sat down on the bed, squashing in between the suitcase and Tamar. "I mean that maybe I'm a little too used to being in the center of things." She spoke slowly, feeling her way. "You know — like the newspaper last year, color war captain, the uniforms —" Shani blushed a little, remembering the shocked dismay she'd felt when she'd discovered that their new uniforms were really surplus from a different school. "Well, you know what I mean. Now this band choir is coming up. I'm sort of glad that I'm not going to be around for the next two weeks when everybody's working on it."

Elisheva, impressed with Shani's candor, nodded her head in silent approval. Tamar, on the other hand, seemed distracted, as if her mind were elsewhere.

"Where are you, Tamar?" Rochel reached out and swatted the bottom of Tamar's foot with her hand.

Tamar jumped. "Huh?"

"I said, where are you?"

"Nowhere, really. Just — thinking." Thinking about the get-together she'd had that Shabbos afternoon…

The girls had come tumbling down the basement stairs, noses pink from the cold and cheeks pink with excitement. Rochel and Elisheva, forewarned, had stayed upstairs or gone visiting. Eighteen out of thirty girls had shown up, and they'd had a marvelous time talking, laughing, even learning a little. Tamar had been gratified to see that Chaya Leah had regained her equilibrium, and the girls had lost a little of their resent-ment. As long as things were working out on their own, Tamar didn't want to say anything; but she couldn't help worrying that the entire issue, once brought out into the open, was a smoldering volcano of violent emotion, merely waiting for the next opportunity to erupt in a tumultuous explosion of anger. If Chaya Leah didn't learn to cope — and the fifth graders didn't learn to separate Rabbi Levi's persona as principal from his role as Chaya Leah's father —

Tamar sighed, then shrugged the matter off. She'd worry about it some other time. Right now, Shani's im-minent departure was infinitely more interesting.

"…really too bad about Nechama," Shani was say-ing. "But I guess I can understand her parents' point of view."

"Sure," Elisheva agreed. "To come back home only three days before a wedding?"

"I'll bet *Nechama* doesn't understand her parents' point of view," Rochel said dryly.

"What are you going to do about Rabbi Levi's as-signment?" Tamar asked her hostess. "By the time you get back, it's going to be only a week and a half before the due date."

A worried crease appeared on Shani's forehead. "I know. Rebbetzin Falovitz said that Raizy and I are excused from regular homework during these two weeks, but major assignments and tests will have to be made up. But it's so hard to buckle down and work when you're away! I've taken off during school time before for family *simchos*, and I always ended up doing any assignments on the last day before I came back."

"You can't do that with this assignment," Rochel pointed out.

"Sure," agreed Elisheva, looking troubled herself. "This is very major." And she didn't even have a topic yet!

"I know," Shani admitted. The worried look deepened. "But at least I'll have Raizy with me. I'm sure she could help me." She shook her head ruefully. "It's going to be hard to do an assignment like this without my father to help me out with some of the —"

She stopped short, her hand flying to cover her mouth and her eyes widening with alarm as she realized what she was saying. She couldn't help cringing as she wished she could snatch the careless, thoughtless words back. How could she say such a thing in front of Rochel? Why did it have to be so easy to wound without intending to?

"Hey, Shani, don't worry," Tamar laughed. "We're managing without our fathers, too!" She sat up on the bed and reached out with her toe to nudge Rochel, who still sat cross-legged on the floor. "Right, Rochel?"

"Right." Rochel's face was carved from stone, her voice wooden and expressionless. "We're managing without our fathers."

Fathers…

Mrs. Kaplan had called again, only half an hour before. She'd laid down an ultimatum: Rochel must come home for Shabbos within the next four weeks.

"I'm sorry, Rochel, but enough is enough. You haven't been home since early September. And Rochel… you can't run away forever. It's time you met Leah Malka and got to know her."

"I met her already," Rochel had said, her voice sullen.

"*Rochel.*" Mrs. Kaplan had sounded exasperated. Then her voice softened as she added, "Rochel, I know how hard it is for you. Second marriages are difficult for everybody. But you're not giving it a chance at all. If you won't even try to adjust, there's no possibility that you ever will…"

"I know," Rochel had mumbled.

"Then you'll come? This Shabbos?"

"I can't this Shabbos," Rochel had said quickly. "Not next Shabbos either. Tests on Sunday."

"And the Shabbos after that?" Mrs. Kaplan's voice had resonated with testiness. "What if you have a test that Sunday, too?" Her patience was evidently wearing thin. Rochel had no choice but to capitulate.

"Okay. Okay. Three Shabbosim from now. All right?"

"All right, Rochel. We'll make arrangements later." A pause, somehow filled with strain and resignation — and maybe a little hope? "Have a *gut voch*, Rochel. Take care."

"*Gut voch*, Ma…"

Shani's anxious voice broke into Rochel's reverie. "I'm sorry, Rochel," she blurted. "I didn't mean to —"

"No problem, Shani. Tamar's right." Rochel stood up and dusted off her hands, her face settling into the familiar lines of the mask of studied indifference she'd worn for the last eighteen months. "We're all managing without our fathers." *I promised myself three years ago that I'd manage. And I will, too — stepfather or no step-father. Stepsister or no stepsister. I will. I WILL!*

Shani watched, troubled, as Rochel strode from the room, her determined footsteps muted by the carpet.

"What was that all about?" Tamar demanded of Shani.

Shani, automatically opening her mouth to reply, almost bit her tongue as she clamped her lips shut. "Nothing," she said lamely, furious with herself. What was *wrong* with her? First she'd thoughtlessly poured salt on Rochel's wounds with her comment, and now she'd almost blurted out the story of Rochel's back-ground to Tamar and Elisheva!

She slammed her suitcase closed with much more force than necessary. "Finished," she said.

"Case closed," Tamar quipped.

"Yeah," Shani said glumly. "Case closed." She only wished that Rochel's situation could be solved as easily.

Elisheva was surprised to discover how awkward she felt in the Baums' home without Shani's steady presence. She felt transported backwards in time, as if she was sitting at that first dinner again, afraid to open her mouth amid all the steady chatter. The classroom, too, felt strange. She was so used to Shani being right in the middle of everything, directing, encouraging, persuading. Even the plans for the band choir, which was largely under Chana Hochberg's direction, seemed to lose much of their impetus in the first few days of Shani's absence.

It wasn't until Wednesday that the girls had managed to adjust to Shani's absence. Chana and Elisheva, seated together during lunchtime, discussed the situation.

"It's just that Shani's always the one who gets things done," Chana mused aloud. "We're all used to Shani getting permission for special activities, Shani doing all the hard work, Shani making sure that every detail is taken care of. But if we want this performance for the first week of Adar, like we planned, we have to get started. We can't just sit around and wait for Shani to come back."

"Okay, so where do we begin?" Elisheva nibbled daintily at her salad. "I understand that Rebbetzin Falovitz made arrangements with Bais Yaakov of Rollenton. What grades do they have?"

"They have ninth through twelfth grade, but we're only involving the ninth and tenth," Chana explained.

"Sure. That makes sense. And where will it be, here or there?"

Chana drummed her fingers on the lunch table. "That's what really has to be decided."

"Oh?"

"Well, yeah. See, Rollenton wants to have us come to them. Don't forget, they came here for the *chidon* at the beginning of the year. But it's going to be pretty expensive to rent a bus for twenty-three girls."

"I see." Elisheva tapped her cheek in thought, a look of concentration settling on her finely-drawn features. "How far is the drive from here to Rollenton?"

"Three hours," Chana sighed. "Why do you think we never merged schools with them? All the little cities are just too far away from each other. When you get right down to it, New York is actually closer."

"In that case, why not get together with one of the New York schools?"

Chana's mouth twisted into a bitter smile. "You really don't know, do you?"

"Know what?"

"Never mind." Chana picked up her sandwich. "Let's just say that large schools aren't usually all too interested in making activities with a high school that consists of a total of twenty-three girls. *Kein yirbu!*"

"What?"

"*Kein yirbu*. It means that our numbers should increase."

"Oh, sure. *Kein yirbu*." Elisheva sighed to herself. So much she didn't know… With an effort, she brought herself back to the original subject. "Okay, so we can't really rent a bus. Is there any other alternative?"

"Not really." Chana chewed a mouthful of sandwich, her eyes unfocused. "Unless we find three or four mothers willing to donate their cars, their driving skills, and an entire day to this. The Rebbetzin suggested it might even be better to stay overnight."

Elisheva leaned forward. "You know, Chana, that's the one part I don't understand in all this. Why is Rebbetzin Falovitz willing to let us miss so much class time for this? I don't mean practicing; we can do that on our time if we had to. But you're talking about a two-day trip!"

Chana put her sandwich down and turned to face Elisheva directly. "The Rebbetzin didn't actually give

me any reasons, but I'll bet I could come up with a few."
She ticked the points off on her fingers. "One: We're
doing this for *tzedakah.* Two: It helps B.Y. High develop a good reputation. Three: Rebbetzin Falovitz always
tells us that a good school has three things — *achdus,
ruach,* and learning. We may not have ended up going
to the Bais Yaakov Convention, but Rebbetzin Falovitz
is going to do her best to make sure that we're not left
out of *everything.*"

"I see." Elisheva stared into her plastic salad con-
tainer.

"Well, we still haven't come up with an answer."
Chana leaned back and stretched. "One thing's excit-
ing, though."

"What?"

"Rollenton has a girl that plays the violin. We've got
you with the flute!"

"And therefore?"

Chana grinned at Elisheva. "And therefore, we're
gonna show those Rollenton girls that Bais Yaakov
High of Bloomfield is every bit as sophisticated as they
are!"

"Oh, sure. Sure." Elisheva smiled at Chana, even
as she mentally rolled her eyes. She was pleased —
proud — that the girls appreciated her musical abilities
so much. But she wasn't interested in competing; she
loved playing for the sake of the music itself.

"One other thing, Elisheva." Chana's eyes twinkled. "Frumi and I have been talking. We want to do a *galus* medley, with an accompanying dance. The only problem is that I want you to be playing the flute and Frumi wants you to be dancing. So we decided that we'll give you a solo on the flute, and then you can go join the dance." She grinned again, her face bright with anticipation. "So what do you think?"

"What do I think?" Elisheva echoed. Her mind dwelled for an uneasy moment on Rabbi Levi's assignment, which she'd barely begun; but memories of her stupendous success at the P'tach parlor meeting merged with fond visions of a performance at which she could incorporate her two great loves — music and dancing — into one wonderful presentation. "I think it's great!"

Eight

"Hi, girls." Mrs. Baum, wiping her hands on a dishtowel, came out of the kitchen to greet Tamar and Elisheva as the wind hustled them into the house. "Where's Rochel?"

"Hi, Mrs. Baum," Tamar said cheerfully as she unwound her scarf. "Rochel went to the Newmans' today. She always goes on Monday afternoons."

"Oh, that's right. I'd forgotten."

"Good afternoon, Mrs. Baum," Elisheva said, her voice decorous as always. "Have you heard any news from Shani?"

"Not today, no. I think I told you she called yesterday. Those young ladies are certainly keeping themselves busy."

"Hard to believe they're actually in Yerushalayim."

Tamar sighed dreamily. "What a dream come true!"

"It is hard to believe, isn't it?" Mrs. Baum agreed. "When Shani called me from Zurich to tell me that the Golds are taking Mimie to a clinic in Yerushalayim, I was absolutely flabbergasted. I'm glad for Shani, though." She turned to Elisheva. "Before I forget — Raizel Koenigsburg called this afternoon. She'd like to speak to you. Would you mind calling her after you've unwound a little? Her number is on the N'shei list."

"Sure." Elisheva hung her jacket neatly in the closet, her eyes betraying her puzzlement. She'd never heard of Raizel Koenigsburg. Who was she?

Half an hour later, Elisheva found out. "We started this *hachnasas kallah* fund in memory of a very special young woman, a *kallah* who was killed in a traffic accident only a few days before her wedding," Mrs. Koenigsburg explained. "We help couples in Eretz Yisrael who are just starting out with linens, towels, dishes, and the like. We are having a fund-raising *melaveh malkah* next week. I was at the P'tach parlor meeting, and your music was just wonderful. Do you think we could possibly ask you to perform for us?"

Elisheva stared at the phone, euphoria bubbling up within her and bursting past her lips. "I'd love to!" she blurted. "Thank you so much for asking me."

"Oh, marvelous. I can't thank you enough. I'll ask Mrs. Baum to drive you over for the performance. Thank you. *Tizku l'mitzvos!*"

A few moments later, Elisheva hung up the phone and floated downstairs to the basement. As usual, Tamar was sitting at the homework table, *sefarim* scattered in all directions as she worked on Rabbi Levi's assignment.

"So, what was it all about?"

Elisheva gave her a dazed and dazzled smile. "I'm performing again. For a *hachnasas kallah melaveh malkah*."

"Hey, great! Congratulations."

"Thank you." Elisheva headed straight for her flute case. "I must start practicing."

Tamar eyed her fellow boarder somewhat doubtfully. Didn't it dawn on Elisheva that Rabbi Levi's assignment was due in just two and a half weeks? She'd barely seen her pick up a *sefer*. She'd seen her pick up her flute often enough, though. If Elisheva wasn't practicing for her solo, she was working on the music she would be playing together with the rest of the band; and whatever spare time she had left after that was spent rehearsing her part in the dance. And now she was going to work on another musical piece as well?

Tamar would have liked to offer to help Elisheva with her work on Rabbi Levi's assignment. She knew how difficult it was for her. But she'd been rebuffed so often, her friendly overtures brushed aside, her warmth cooled by Elisheva's proper dignity. By now, Tamar felt it would be better not to interfere. If Elisheva wanted her help, she'd surely ask for it; but Tamar didn't intend to be refused again.

She glanced across the room. Elisheva had already assembled the collapsible music stand and was looking through sheets of music, scanning the notes with a practiced eye. Finding one that met her satisfaction, she set the sheet music on the stand, straightened, and raised the flute to her lips.

Elisheva was one busy musician, all right. But Tamar wondered — must inattentiveness to schoolwork be the price for performing beautiful music?

"All right, girls, it's Wednesday, so we'll stop here." Rabbi Levi closed his Chumash and kissed it. "With only two weeks left for your assignment, I'm sure many of you have questions you'd like to ask. We will follow the same format as we did last week; you may all work quietly at your desks. I will call you up, one at a time, to deal with any difficulties you may have." He sat down at his desk — the only time he ever seemed to actually sit down was during these consultations — and held a pen poised in his hand. "Those of you who wish to speak to me, please raise your hand."

Hands shot up all over the room. Rabbi Levi's eyes flicked up, then down to his notebook as he jotted down the name of each girl. Elisheva, however, did not raise her hand; she carefully turned the pages of her notebook, quailing at the vast number of empty pages. How could she tell Rabbi Levi that she needed help because she'd barely gotten started?

She seemed to be so busy lately. The performance in Adar — both her solo, the dance, and the band itself — took up so much time. With Shani temporarily out of the picture, Elisheva had found herself, quite unexpectedly, right in the center of everything. Costumes, transportation, rehearsals — it seemed that every aspect of the performance demanded her attention. They'd managed to rent two large vans at a very reasonable price; Bashie Klein and Naomi Hochner, two of the older girls in the community, had volunteered to drive the girls to Rollenton and act as chaperones. Shula Goldman had written a small play that would serve to introduce each song in the medley; not actually narration, but two-minute skits explaining what each song was about. The entire performance blended together beautifully. Elisheva's letters home were filled with glowing descriptions and excited comments.

And yet…and yet…

It frightened her to think of how far behind she was lagging in her schoolwork. She hadn't actually neglected anything, but she hadn't really advanced in the last three weeks, either. And as Rabbi Levi had pointed out just a few days ago, one either progressed or regressed;

there is no such thing as standing still. Elisheva did not like to think about which one probably applied to her right now.

But what could she do? Refuse to perform at the *hachnasas kallah melaveh malkah*? Back out of the band choir production when everyone was counting on her to preserve the honor of B.Y. High with her flute?

She expressed her doubts to Chana at their daily meeting at lunch.

"Don't worry about it, Elisheva," Chana said easily. "We're all more or less in the same boat. We're all juggling schoolwork with practices. You'll be fine."

"But — Rabbi Levi's big assignment. I have so much left to do. And there's only two weeks. What if —"

"Uh uh." Chana wiggled a finger at her. "No 'what if's allowed, Elisheva. If you start with the 'what if's, we'll never do anything. Just relax a little. It'll be fine."

"If you say so." Elisheva sighed. Perhaps it would be better if she just kept her doubts to herself. Frumi Scharf had said much the same thing yesterday, when Elisheva had brought up the subject during dance practice: "Don't worry so much, Elisheva. It'll be fine."

Maybe it would be, too. Elisheva just wished that she could be as sure as everyone else.

"Hey, Elisheva! Shani's on the pay phone!" Tamar dashed over to the ninth graders' table.

"Shani? She's back in Bloomfield?" Elisheva stood up and pushed her chair back.

"Yeah. She got home about twenty minutes ago. Come on!"

The two girls hurried over to the pay phone out in the hallway, followed by half of their classmates. Rochel had the receiver clamped tightly against her right ear and her hand pressed tightly against her left ear in a futile attempt to block out the noisy hallway. "That's amazing…no kidding…unbelievable…"

Tamar yanked impatiently on her sleeve. "*Nu*, Rochel? Let Elisheva have a turn."

"Okay, okay…" Reluctantly, Rochel turned the phone over to Elisheva, who momentarily held the receiver away from her ear at Shani's overly loud voice.

"What's going on?" Chana demanded of Rochel, who turned away from the phone with a misty-eyed smile.

"Mimie Gold is walking," she answered simply.

"Oh, wow. *Baruch Hashem!*" They all gathered around the phone, laughing and talking, getting all the incredible details of Mimie's miraculous first steps at the Kosel. The noise rose to an overwhelming crescendo, until —

"*What is going on here?*"

The girls fell silent, shocked. Rebbetzin Falovitz, their beloved principal, stood framed in the hallway entrance, her gray eyes clouded with disapproval.

She spoke softly into a heavy, thick silence. "I think my high school girls have forgotten how to behave." Her voice was sad, disappointed, making the girls feel ten times worse than an ordinary scolding.

Quietly, the subdued girls dispersed, unable to meet the Rebbetzin's gaze. Without talking, they made their way back to the ninth-grade classroom.

An uncomfortable silence lingered over the class for the rest of the afternoon. Rebbetzin Falovitz almost *never* had to scold them. It cast a pall over the girls, and any conversations were conducted in murmurs and undertones, with quick, furtive glances in all directions.

Rochel, Elisheva, and Tamar discussed it as they walked home that afternoon, eager to see Shani again and hear a detailed, firsthand account of her trip to Zurich and Yerushalayim.

"Can you imagine that scene taking place in a public school?" Tamar mused. "One little sentence, and the Rebbetzin had us practically in tears."

Elisheva nodded. "Yes. She's a very special woman."

Rochel kicked at the dirty, blackened slush lying in sullen heaps at the edges of the sidewalk. "Yeah, well, we *were* being pretty noisy."

"We'll just have to work on it, that's all," Elisheva declared, her lilting voice firm with resolve.

Tamar nodded thoughtfully. She readily admitted that she had probably been talking — and shrieking —

the loudest. She resolved once more to reserve the more rambunctious side of her nature for more appropriate moments.

The appropriate moment presented itself the following Sunday afternoon, when she met her fifth graders at the Bloomfield roller rink during Ladies' Hour. None of them needed to cling to the rail for support while skating, but none of them could match Tamar's antics, either.

Tamar knew she had a rather wide streak of flamboyancy. She had long since given up on trying to determine how much derived from her innate sense of pride in her accomplishments, and how much was a direct result of her understanding that younger children are more likely to admire and emulate an older girl who is a good athlete. For example, she knew she never would have been able to convince her saucy fifth graders in Kedzie to come hear about the parashah on Shabbos if she hadn't won their admiration first by hitting three home runs in a row in a baseball game. Now, as she demonstrated figure-eights, backwards skating, speed skating, and all the other little tricks she'd learned over the years, she saw the same fascination stamped on the faces of these Bais Yaakov of Bloomfield girls. Yes, the same formula she'd used in Kedzie would work here, too. Snowball fights, *machanayim* games, roller skating — she knew they would want to copy her. And if she showed an equal enthusiasm for learning, they would emulate that, as well.

"Tamar, like this?" Chaya Leah's strokes were clumsy, but she made her way around the rink well enough.

"Tamar, show me…"

"Look, Tamar, I'm doing it!" Shosh waved her arms in triumph.

Sima Yehudis, a girl with expressive brown eyes and a pixie haircut, struggled to keep her balance. Tamar glided smoothly across the rink, her skates moving in lazy, slow strokes. "C'mon, Simie," she laughed, grabbing the girl's hand. "Let's you and me have a go at it together!"

Shades of Elisheva, Tamar thought to herself with a grin.

Sima Yehudis glowed. "Thanks, Tamar." Her embarrassment at her ineptitude vanished in the pride of skating together with this fascinating ninth grader.

After forty minutes, Tamar was ready for a breather. Her skates hissed to a stop as she moved off the rink, flopping down gracelessly onto one of the benches nearby. Several girls sat down near her, rolling their skates aimlessly along the carpet, while others remained on the rink and continued to skate.

"I'm exhausted," she declared to her attentive audience, rolling her eyes dramatically. "I don't think I could move another inch."

"Sure you could," Bracha laughed.

"Well, maybe in the direction of Ben-Levi's pizza shop," Tamar agreed with a wink.

"As long as it's not in the direction of school," a girl Tamar had identified as Fraydie added rather morosely. A few more girls left the rink and approached the group.

"Not *all* school is bad," Tamar pointed out. "Math isn't one of my favorites, though."

"Or geography."

"Or spelling."

"Or history."

"Or tests or homework."

"Or punishment assignments!"

This last, unlike the other jocular comments, burst out with the force of frustration. Tamar sat up, feeling concerned.

"What happened?" she asked quietly.

Tamar didn't recognize the girl who had spoken, but Shevi broke in with an explanation. "Rabbi Levi didn't just take away our field trip. He gave us this huge assignment to do. It's just not fair!"

"It's not Rabbi *Levi*," the first girl muttered snidely. "It's Rabbi *Meanie*."

Tamar's dark eyes suddenly flashed fire. "That's *chutzpahdik*," she said, the iciness of her voice a vivid contrast to the hot anger in her face.

The girl bit her lip and turned away, but Tamar reached out and grabbed her arm. The other girls stared at Tamar, riveted. Nobody noticed Chaya Leah leave the rink and make her way toward them.

"Listen…what's your name?"

"Malka."

"Listen, Malka. I'm not perfect any more than you are. I've gotten punishments for things I've done, and I've been angry at teachers. But you can't speak about a teacher — especially your principal — like that. No matter how resentful you might be, no matter how unfair you think a situation is, you can't forget to treat your teachers with the proper respect. Okay?"

Malka hesitated; then a tentative smile twitched at the corner of her mouth. "Okay."

"Good." Tamar leaned back and grinned at her, and the tension eased.

"I guess we really did deserve it, anyway," Shosh sighed.

"Oh?"

"Yeah. You see…we…um…"

"Cheated," Bracha finished.

"What?" Tamar stared.

"We had an Israeli substitute who couldn't really read English. We wrote all the answers to a quiz on the blackboard on the side of the room and told her that it was stuff from the English teacher."

"I…see," Tamar managed.

"But Rabbi Levi came into the room in the middle of the quiz to check how we were getting on with the sub, and he figured out what we were doing." Shevi slouched down on the bench. "Boy, was he mad!"

Nobody seemed to realize that Chaya Leah was standing behind the group, her face pale as she listened to the conversation.

"I guess Rabbi Levi knows how to read English," Tamar said dryly. "So tell me, was the cheating worth it?"

"It would have been, if Rabbi Levi hadn't caught us," Malka muttered.

Tamar turned her head and caught sight of Chaya Leah. She reached out and took her hand. "No," she said, speaking to Malka but looking directly at Chaya Leah. "Cheating is *never* worth it."

Nine

ochel trudged toward the Baums' house, her head bent against the wind and her brown hair whipping in her face. She hated walking in the dark; the stars glittered coldly, reflections of ice crystals in a black sky, driving home her feelings of loneliness, of standing remote from the rest of the world.

Each Monday was the same. Instead of going home with Tamar and Elisheva, she walked home with little Adina Newman and stayed for over an hour, folding laundry, feeding the kids supper, just talking with Mrs. Newman with the deep sense of understanding each other.

How could they not? The Newmans knew her well by now; she was practically part of the family, an integral part of the Newmans' healing process after the loss of their father.

Irony of ironies, she thought bitterly. *I had to find another little girl whose father died in order to feel at home.*

She knew such thoughts were unfair to herself, to her mother, to her family — and yes, to her stepfather, whether she wanted to admit it or not. But logic was little comfort. This coming Shabbos loomed before her, silent and menacing. The Shabbos that had seemed so far off when Shani had been packing to leave was suddenly only five days away.

Her steps quickened as she neared the Baums' home, eager to reach the sanctuary of warmth and light. Her feet scuffled on the ice-rimmed pavement as she mounted the steps and rang the bell before pushing the door open.

She shook out her coat and scarf before hanging it on a hook near the door. They were still too wet to hang in the closet; she'd have to take care of that later. Warm, appetizing smells drifted from the kitchen, beckoning her to enter.

Shani stood near the table, folding napkins. She looked up as Rochel came in. "Hi," she greeted her. "How'd it go today?"

"Fine." Rochel crossed over to the stove and held her red, chapped hands over the steaming pot.

"It's gotten colder out there, huh?"

"Yeah."

Shani sighed to herself. She ought to know by now that Rochel was usually monosyllabic after her Monday evenings with the Newmans. She couldn't help trying, though.

"I was just talking to Elisheva," she remarked, trying to fill the oppressive silence hanging over the kitchen. "They've really planned something special for this *erev shirah*. Just about everyone's involved in it, aren't they?"

Rochel shrugged.

Shani frowned, folded one last napkin, and moved closer to the stove. "Are *you*?" she asked pointedly.

"No."

Shani leaned against the *fleishig* counter, her face troubled. "Why not?"

Rochel shrugged again. "I guess I'm not all that interested in seeing another hick town."

Shani's eyes flashed for a moment before she regained control. "We're *all* going, Rochel. I'm not part of the performance — I missed too much when I was away — but I'm going along. I can help — with costumes, curtains, whatever's needed. Why don't you want to come along?"

"I just don't." Her voice was flat, like a nail scraping against a stone.

"Rochel —"

"No, Shani." Rochel dropped her hands to her sides. "Forget it." She turned on her heel and walked toward the basement door without looking back. She'd thought that Shani knew better than that by now.

The sounds of Elisheva's flute drifted up the stairs. Rochel grimaced to herself. Her roommate's regular daily half hour of practice didn't bother her that much, but three hours of constant classical music was just a little too much for her. Even regular Jewish music sounded highbrow on the flute. And with Elisheva practicing her solo, her part in the band choir, *and* the piece she would be performing at a *hachnasas kallah* activity — it all added up to a lot of time spent with Rochel's headphones jammed over her ears.

Tamar exchanged a look of long-suffering with Rochel as she came down the stairs. "Welcome to the Conrad Symphony Orchestra, Rochel," she quipped with a weary grin.

"Yeah, right." Rochel strode over to her bed, pulled her Walkman out from under her pillow, and slipped the headphones on with a feeling of relief. She pushed the "play" button, and turned the volume on as high as it could go. Then, with Avi Shoham blasting familiarly and comfortably in her eardrums, she went over to her shelf, pulled out her notebook and Chumash, and sat down next to Tamar at the table.

"How's it coming?" Tamar half-shouted, nodding at Rochel's notebook.

Rochel deliberately spoke in a low voice, knowing she had a tendency to speak loudly when she was listening to music on her Walkman. "My research is just about done. I want to make an outline now, and then I'll be able to write it up."

"Me, too." Tamar grinned and patted her notebook affectionately. "I think this is the best paper I've ever done for an assignment like this. I hope I get a good mark…"

Elisheva overheard the remark as she paused to turn a page. She looked up, stung; the casual comment cut her to the quick. Her face clouded over as she lowered her flute. Maybe it was the best paper Tamar had ever done, but her own work was so sketchy. How would she possibly finish on time?

Tamar looked up with surprise as the music came to an abrupt halt. "Finished?"

"Yes," Elisheva mumbled, her face flushed. Her movements were jerky as she disassembled the flute and put it away. The assignment was due a week from Wednesday; she could no longer afford the luxury of procrastination. She had to put aside her music and get to work — now.

But as Elisheva joined Tamar and Rochel at the table and opened her own notebook, the stark contrast between her scanty jottings and the organized notes of the others was painfully obvious. She kept sneaking glances at the other two, longing to somehow bridge the yawning gap between their vast knowledge and her weak background. And Tamar! How could she look so *happy* as she scribbled and erased, crossing out and revising sentences? How could she possibly enjoy this so much?

She'd barely sketched out the beginnings of an outline when Shani's voice came floating down the stairs. "Suppertime!"

Tamar gave a little sigh, then reached out and tugged Rochel's sleeve. Rochel glanced at her, startled, then pulled the headphones off her ears. "What is it? What's wrong?"

"The voice from above." Tamar grinned at Rochel, who winked back. "And I don't know about you, but I'm starved. Coming?"

"Yeah, sure." Rochel shoved her chair back and stood. She tossed her Walkman onto her upper bunk and headed upstairs.

Tamar stood up, too, giving her notebook one last thoughtful glance before closing it. She took three steps toward the stairs, then turned back to look at Elisheva.

"What's wrong, Elisheva? Aren't you coming?"

Elisheva looked up, and something flashed in her eyes — desperation? Panic? Then she blinked, and the glint faded away. "Sure, I'm coming," she said, her voice dull. She stood up, moving slowly and heavily, as if she were underwater, and she walked carefully, her feet feeling their way along the floor.

Tamar watched, puzzled, then followed her up the stairs. Elisheva wouldn't tell her what was wrong — not yet. Only time would tell.

Suri Nadel's basement shimmered with concentration. Michal Elias, Rivka Pollack, Shayna Weiss, Rochi Davis, and Rivki Kuperman stood together in a half-circle, hands clasped loosely behind their backs and eyes half-closed as they sang. Chana Hochberg, her fingers flowing over the keyboard of her electric organ, looked up frequently, singing along with the choir in an undertone. Suri Nadel tapped softly on the drums, merely holding the beat in this slow, gentle song, while Bayla Rosner's fingers flicked expertly on the strings of her guitar. Elisheva's flute carried the melody, with Shoshanah Klein's triangle adding a chime of emphasis.

The final chords of the song died away. The ten girls exchanged looks of unqualified approval.

"Perfect," Chana said softly, voicing the thought for them all. "Absolutely perfect."

Michal nodded, her mouth curving upward in a smile. "Do you want to go over it again?"

"No, I think we can call it quits for now." Chana turned off her Casio, stood up, and shook her hands vigorously. "It's been an hour already, and I think I'm not the only one who's getting tired."

"You said it," grinned Suri, bringing her drumsticks down on the cymbals with a crash for emphasis.

"So when do we meet again?" Rochi asked as she poured herself a glass of orange juice from the pitcher on the nearby table.

Chana tugged at a loose strand of hair, biting her lip as she frowned in thought. "We can't impose too much on Mrs. Nadel," she mused aloud. "And we have to have the practices here, since it's too hard for Suri to bring the drums to somebody else's house."

"That's for sure." Suri punctuated her heartfelt agreement with another clash of the cymbals.

"So how about next week? Or do you think we need another practice before that?" Chana frowned, her fingers running lightly along the keys of the Casio. "If it was just a regular choir, this wouldn't be such a problem; we could just have the piano in school. But the whole point of this is supposed to be the music, and we need to rehearse together." She glanced around at the others, her face mirroring her indecision. "Any ideas?"

"I think we should wait until next Wednesday night," Rivka Pollack suggested.

"Why specifically next Wednesday night?"

Rivka's eyes twinkled. "Because then we'll all have turned in Rabbi Levi's assignment that day, and we won't have it hanging over our heads anymore."

"I second the motion," said Elisheva, her voice surprisingly full of feeling.

Michal grinned. "Yeah, I think Rivka's right." She looked around at the others. "Agreed?"

Heads nodded around the room. "I'll be glad when that assignment is turned in," Shoshanah sighed. "Then we can all just work on this without having to worry anymore."

"Right." Suri stretched and yawned.

"Is that a hint, Suri?" Chana teased.

"Yeah, I guess so." Suri grinned without a trace of embarrassment.

"Okay, then," Chana laughed back. "Let's all leave Suri to go to sleep."

Ten girls drifted upstairs, talking quietly — it was pretty late, and the Nadel children had long since gone to sleep. Nine of them struggled into coats, wrapped instruments securely against the cold, and made their way home. Rivka and Chana, who lived too far away to walk, waited for Mrs. Hochberg to come pick them up and take them home. Shayna, Bayla, and Elisheva walked down the quiet street together. The air seemed wrapped in stillness, great gray clouds drifting silently against a background of winking stars. It seemed natural to speak in hushed whispers in the still night.

"How are you doing on your paper?" Shayna asked Bayla as she huddled deeply into her coat.

"I'm just about done," Bayla replied, her voice tinged with a soft sound of relief. "I just have to copy it and write down all the footnotes. How about you?"

"I want to go over it again before I write it up." Shayna sighed. "Boy, will I be glad when this is over. How about you, Elisheva?"

"I still have a bit more to go," Elisheva said after a moment's hesitation. "I think I'll be finished on time." Her tone left no room for further discussion, and the others graciously took the hint. They walked on in silence, their footsteps loud against the quiet, until they reached the Baums' home and dropped Elisheva off.

"Good night, Elisheva. See you tomorrow!" The two girls waved and hurried down the street and around the corner, the mist of their breathing dissipating into the cold night air.

Elisheva mounted the three steps and let herself into the house with the key. Here, too, all was quiet; the Baums must be upstairs, and by ten thirty at night, Rochel and Tamar would probably be winding down and unwilling to venture upstairs. Elisheva hung up her coat, then walked through the kitchen on silent feet and down the steps to the basement.

The room was dim and soft with the sound of hushed, even breathing. Rochel was asleep, a mass of brown hair spread across her pillow. Even in slumber, the corners of her mouth turned down slightly, her forehead furrowed in frowning thought. Tamar lay on the lower bunk, her blanket pulled up to her shoulders, reading a book by the light of the small lamp on the table. She glanced up as Elisheva came in on tiptoes, clutching her precious flute case in her hand.

"Hi," Tamar greeted softly, keeping her voice low. "How did the practice go?"

"Pretty good, thanks." Elisheva crossed the room and deposited her flute case on her shelf. "It takes a lot of practice to get us all playing on the same key at the same time. Some people seem to think all you have to do is say, 'and a one, and a two, and a three,' but it's a lot harder than that. Michal was there tonight, too, so we had the singing to accompany us."

"Does that make it harder or easier?"

"It depends, really. Sometimes I think we sort of keep each other on key; sometimes I think it just makes things more difficult. It's hard to say." Elisheva gathered her nightgown and robe together, then walked into the bathroom and shut the door.

Tamar stared thoughtfully at the closed door. She knew Elisheva well enough by now to tell that something was bothering her, and bothering her a lot. She also suspected that it had something to do with Rabbi Levi's big Chumash assignment, due exactly one week from tonight. Tamar had just about finished hers already; she still planned to go over it again, but the research was complete, and she'd already made a rough draft of her final paper. Rochel, too, was just about finished, and Shani, while she was still somewhat behind after her sojourn in Zurich and Yerushalayim, seemed confident that she'd be finished on time.

But Elisheva? Elisheva spent so much time practicing on her flute that little time was left for schoolwork. And Tamar couldn't help remembering that glint of panic that she'd spotted in Elisheva's eyes two nights ago…

But Elisheva had lines that no one could cross. Tamar had been rebuffed, ever so politely, enough times to realize that. Much as she wanted to offer Elisheva her assistance, she was just going to have to wait for her South African roommate to make the first move.

"Rochel, you have a phone call!" Yitzy's voice filtered down the stairs. "It's from New York."

Rochel stiffened visibly. She cast an almost frightened glance at the phone hanging on the wall near the washing machine. Her steps were jerky as she walked toward it, the tip of her tongue wetting ash-dry lips.

Elisheva forced herself to avert her eyes. She still didn't know what secret Rochel harbored, and she didn't want to invade on her privacy, but the sight of tough, stubborn Rochel Kaplan looking so unnerved was hard to take. She caught Tamar's eye and jerked her head toward the stairs. Silently, the two girls left the room, leaving Rochel alone with the telephone.

Rochel always hated to get phone calls from home. It was like someone ripping the scabs off freshly healing wounds, hammering home the reality of what awaited her, of what was impossible to escape. But this Thursday night, the phone was a cobra coiled and ready to strike a fatal blow to the brave front Rochel presented to the world. "Hello?" She couldn't stop her voice from quavering.

"Hello, Rochel."

Him.

"How are you doing?"

"Fine, *baruch Hashem*," Rochel managed. She could not bring herself to say, *How are you?*

"We wanted to make plans to come and pick you up," Mr. Kaplan said, his voice deliberately calm and pleasant. "Winter Fridays are short, and it's almost a two-hour drive. Your mother wanted to come up and get you herself, but we'll have to see what happens; she might not be able to get away."

"Oh," Rochel croaked.

"At any rate, one of us will probably arrive in Bloomfield before noon." Mr. Kaplan paused for a moment, then said carefully, "If it turns out that I come in to pick you up, I do not think I should come to the Bais Yaakov building. Can you be at the Baums' at lunchtime?"

"Yes. Yes, I can." *And thank you. Thank you for not coming to Bais Yaakov. Thank you for not making me face hundreds of prying, greedy eyes.*

"Good. Good." Mr. Kaplan paused again, and Rochel couldn't help thinking that he had somehow heard her thoughts. "We're all very glad you're coming home this Shabbos, Rochel. Leah Malka, especially, is looking forward to meeting you again."

"That's nice." The words were flat, dropped from a vast distance into a pond of stagnant water, stirring up unpleasant thoughts and disturbing those memories that were better left alone.

"Well…" Mr. Kaplan coughed. "Perhaps it would be better if we talked after you came back to New York. Could I possibly speak to Dr. Baum?"

"Certainly. Just a minute, please." Rochel's words were polite, but her voice betrayed her relief at the chance to avoid the further strain of speaking with her stepfather. She ran up the steps two at a time and burst into the kitchen, where Dr. and Mrs. Baum chatted quietly over mugs of steaming coffee.

"Dr. Baum, could you please pick up the phone?"

"Yes, of course." Dr. Baum rose and stepped to the phone. "Who is it?"

Rochel swallowed, then steeled herself to say it. "My...father." The word came out as a choked sob, and she turned and fled back downstairs to the sanctuary of her room.

Dr. and Mrs. Baum exchanged rueful glances. Did Rochel know that Rabbi Levi and Rebbetzin Falovitz had informed them of her background?

Shaking his head slowly, Dr. Baum lifted the receiver and spoke. "Hello, Mr. Kaplan? Yes, *aleichem shalom*... No, not at all. Certainly... Oh, really? I see... Hmmm. No, I think I might be able to help you. I purchased some new equipment recently, and my old oxygen masks are hardly obsolete..."

Shani, followed by Tamar and Elisheva, came trailing downstairs and into the kitchen. "Hi, Mommy," she greeted her mother. "Is Rochel off the phone ye —"

"Shhh!" Mrs. Baum pointed to her husband, who was still busy talking.

"...well, I intend to be in my office this Sunday. Why don't you come pick the equipment up then?" Dr. Baum snapped his fingers. "In fact, I can save you an extra trip that way. Bring Rochel with you to my office when you come for the equipment, and then she can come back to Bloomfield with me."

Shani, whose jaw had hung loose as she listened, made a dive for her father.

"I'll come along!" she hissed.

"Excuse me, please." Dr. Baum lowered the phone and covered the mouthpiece with one hand. "What was that, Shani?"

"I'll come along with you." The words tumbled out of her mouth in her eagerness. "That way Rochel will have me in the car on the way home."

Dr. Baum's eyebrows arched upwards. "Are you sure?"

"Yes!"

"Well…" Dr. Baum lifted the phone again. "My daughter Shani has offered to come along with me into New York, so Rochel won't be alone. If you…" He stopped short and listened, a resigned look coming into his eyes. "Yes, I see. I suppose I should have thought of that myself. No, I understand. It's a highly sensitive… What? All right, we'll be in touch. We still might be able to work something out and spare you the trip. No, thank you. Yes. Have a good Shabbos." He hung up.

"What's wrong?" Shani demanded.

Dr. Baum looked at his daughter with narrowed eyes. "It won't work out, Shani. Let's just leave it at that."

"But *why*?" Shani was dying to meet Rochel's step-father. Here was a perfect opportunity! Why couldn't she go?

"Shani…because I said so." Dr. Baum's eyes bored into hers.

Shani closed her mouth in a hurry. As long as she could remember, that answer had been her parents' final, ultimate admonition to stop asking questions and just accept their dictums and decisions without argument. "Sorry," she said meekly.

Tamar and Elisheva, standing just within the doorway, had watched the proceedings with a great deal of curiosity. There was nothing they could ask in front of Shani's parents, though. They would have to wait for an opportunity to speak to Shani alone.

"Well," Tamar said with exaggerated casualness, "I think we'd better go downstairs. Unless you need some erev Shabbos help, Mrs. Baum?"

Mrs. Baum shook her head, her blue eyes smiling more than her mouth. "Thank you, Tamar, but everything seems to be pretty taken care of."

"Okay, then." Tamar sauntered across the kitchen, pulling a bemused Elisheva along. "G'night, all!"

"What was that about?" Elisheva murmured to her as they went downstairs.

"Tell you later," Tamar said vaguely. It was obvious that the conversation had something to do with Rochel; it was equally obvious that it was not going to be easy to find out what was going on. The answer, whatever it was, would just have to wait.

Ten

The sound of soft, even breathing filled the room, mocking her inability to sleep. The red numbers of Tamar's alarm clock glowed spitefully in the darkness; even as she watched, they flickered and changed from 1:59 to 2:00.

Rochel turned over onto her stomach. Two o'clock in the morning, and she was wide awake. How could she sleep when her small carry-on bag was filled with Shabbos paraphernalia, knowing that in another ten hours she would be on her way to Brooklyn?

She quietly slipped down from her bunk bed, moving slowly to avoid any loud creaks that might wake up Tamar or Elisheva. Her feet slid into her slippers, and she padded over to the clothes rod to get her robe. She cast one swift glance back at her slumbering roommates before climbing the stairs to the kitchen.

Her breathing sounded noisy in the silence. The faint, subliminal hum of the refrigerator motor traced a soft counterpart to the whispered ticking of the kitchen clock. The room was dark, with only a faint hint of moonlight peeking through the folds of the closed curtains and the fainter glow of the outside porch light filtering in from the hallway. She moved instinctively around the counter in the darkness, taking the kettle off the stove and filling it with water from the sink. She turned the flame on high and set the kettle back down before turning back to sit at the kitchen table.

She cupped her chin in her hands as she stared unseeingly at the kitchen wall, lost in somber contemplation of the inevitable. Thoughts chased themselves wildly around her mind, like dead autumn leaves skittering in a sudden gust of wind. The soft hissing from the kettle grew louder, and she rose to turn the fire off before the whistling began.

As she poured milk into her steaming cocoa, a thin sliver of light darted down the steps leading upstairs. Soft footsteps sounded, and Shani came into view, a powder-blue robe clutched tightly around her.

"Did I wake you up?" Rochel whispered.

Shani shook her head, her eyes red from lack of sleep and her blond hair tousled. "No," she whispered back. "I woke up about half an hour ago, and I couldn't fall asleep again."

"Oh." Rochel gestured at the kettle, steam still wafting upwards. "Want cocoa?"

"Yeah. Thanks."

The two girls sat quietly at the table, bound together by two moments: a moment of quiet understanding in Shani's bedroom, and a moment of shocked comprehension in a second-grade classroom. For several minutes, they said nothing, sipping the hot cocoa and eyeing each other over the rims of their mugs as their vision adjusted to the dim light of the kitchen.

Shani finally broke the silence. "I wanted to be able to talk to you, Rochel. That's the real reason I came downstairs."

"Oh?"

"You know my father spoke to —?" She couldn't bring herself to finish the sentence.

"Yeah."

"I heard part of the conversation." Shani dropped her gaze, tracing a pattern on the kitchen table with her finger. "I didn't really understand it, but — I think your — your —"

"Stepfather," Rochel said for her flatly.

"Yeah. Your — stepfather." Shani coughed. "Well, he's getting something from my father on Sunday, and my father offered to take you home from his office, so I said maybe I could come, too…"

Rochel's eyes gleamed in the darkness. "You wanted to come along, huh? Do a little sightseeing at the dentist's office?"

Shani hoped the light was too dim for Rochel to see her blush. "I-I guess it wasn't very nice of me. When you put it that way… But…"

"Right." Rochel leaned back and put her mug down on the table with a soft thump. "So what did your father say?"

"Well, it was sort of strange. At first he thought it was okay, but then he relayed the offer over the phone, and your — um — stepfather must have said no for some reason. Like I said, it was weird. My father apologized for not thinking, and then he wouldn't give me any explanation."

"Oh." The syllable contained a wealth of understanding. Rochel had no trouble figuring out why Shmuel Kaplan had objected; he must have displayed the same sensitivity as he had when he recognized that Rochel would not want her stepfather showing up at the Bais Yaakov building.

But now, no matter how illogical she knew it might be, Rochel felt a slow swell of anger building up within her. She didn't want him to protect her. She could protect herself. And besides, didn't Shani know already?

What difference would it make if she saw Rochel's stepfather?

"If you really want to go along, Shani, I don't see any reason why you shouldn't."

Shani sat up straight. "Do you mean it?"

Rochel lifted her mug and drank the last of the cocoa. "Sure, why not? I don't mind providing you with a little entertainment."

Shani flushed again. "That's not fair, Rochel…"

"No, you're right, it's not. But who said I promised to be fair?"

"But that's not the point, Rochel. Okay, I'll admit it. I *am* curious to see what he looks like. But I don't think I'm so morbid that I'd want to drag myself to New York on a Sunday afternoon just for that, unless —" Shani took a deep breath before she finished her sentence. "— unless I was also doing it for you."

Rochel turned the empty mug around in her hands, brown eyes holding Shani's blue ones in an unwinking gaze. After a long moment, one corner of her mouth lifted.

"All right, Shani Baum." She put down the mug and held her hand out across the table. "Truce."

Once again, the basement room buzzed with activity. Only now, with Rochel away in Brooklyn, it was Tamar who French-braided Elisheva's hair, while Shani

fussed over which outfit she should wear for her performance at the *hachnasas kallah melaveh malkah.*

There was another difference, so subtle it escaped
Tamar and Shani's notice. Elisheva was certainly nervous, hands clasped tightly together to conceal the trem-
ors, but this time, her anxiety stemmed from an entirely
different source: Rabbi Levi's Chumash assignment.

The due date was only four days away. True, once
this performance was over, she would have no more
official practices until after the paper had already been
handed in to Rabbi Levi. She would only need to devote
her usual half hour to her music, giving her that much
more time to work on her paper. But how — *how* would
she manage? Even if she struggled and struggled, how
could she possibly ever finish on time?

Tamar's paper was finished already; she merely
needed to rewrite it — in Hebrew, no less! Rochel's,
too, was complete, also written in Hebrew. Elisheva
didn't know what language Shani had used, but she did
know that all Shani had left to do was polish her rough
draft into a neat composition. And Elisheva? She had
an outline and the beginnings of several paragraphs,
in English, scribbled frantically in her notebook. Small
wonder, then, that her stomach churned and icy fingers
groped along her veins. How could she possibly worry
about her performance when she was so worried about
the assignment?

If only there was something she could do…if only there was some way she could get help…

"There!" Tamar slipped the ponytail holder off her wrist and fastened it into place. "It's a corn braid, really, not a French braid. I did it backwards."

"Let's see." Elisheva went into the bathroom, carrying her pocket mirror in her hand, and angled it so she could see the back of her head. "Oh! It's really pretty, Tamar. Thank you."

Tamar grinned. "All part of the service," she replied, trying to mimic Rochel's clipped tones.

Elisheva smiled back as best as she could, then took the outfit the three of them had chosen and closed the bathroom door so she could change.

The evening passed in much the same fashion as it had a few weeks before at the P'tach parlor meeting. Shani and Tamar accompanied Elisheva to the Koenigsburg residence. Elisheva recognized many faces from her performance at the Chinns'. Heartened at knowing she had a receptive audience, Elisheva sternly banished the sick feelings of nervousness and raised her flute to her lips.

Once again, the soaring notes of the flute bore her upwards, lifting her on high to float amid vast clouds of music in a cotton-pink sea. Faces blurred, and her vision was encompassed by the black and white pages of her sheet music. Shani and Tamar stood in the back, watching and listening with fond pride as Elisheva poured her heart into her flute.

As the last notes faded away, Elisheva looked up, her eyes shining and her cheeks flushed with exertion. There was an infinitesimal pause, and then came thunderous applause, with Tamar and Shani enthusiastically contributing their share.

This time, Tamar felt no bitterness, no envy of the adulation Elisheva received. She did not need to. The work she had done with her fifth graders, the get-together with its emphasis on *shemiras halashon* that had become a regular fixture of their Shabbos afternoons, the help she had given Chaya Leah Levi in separating herself from the persona of the principal's daughter — Tamar was content in the knowledge that she was able to make her mark in Bloomfield in her own fashion, even as Elisheva was able to in hers.

Later, as the two boarders settled down for the night, Tamar remarked, "Too bad Rochel wasn't here tonight. You really did a beautiful job."

"Thanks." Elisheva's smile was a little tremulous.

Tamar weighed the situation carefully. She desperately wanted to offer Elisheva her help, but she'd been rebuffed so often that she felt sure that Elisheva would consider any offers insulting. At the same time, however, maybe Elisheva *did* want some assistance at this point. It was painfully obvious that

Elisheva was nearly drowning in a welter of panic, overwhelmed and unable to complete her assignment. If she hadn't spent so much time practicing for her various performances, maybe she would have been able to manage; but now, with the paper due in four short days, Elisheva was faced with a deadline and no way to meet it.

Carefully, picking her way through a field mined with potential disaster, Tamar made a supposedly casual observation. "I guess now that this performance is over, you'll have a little more time to work on Rabbi Levi's assignment."

Elisheva jumped. "Sure," she croaked, refusing to meet Tamar's gaze.

Tamar waited, and Elisheva finally turned her head to look her directly in the eye. "I don't know what to do," she confessed, her voice low and strained. "I have so much work left. I don't see how I'll ever finish on time."

"Maybe I can help." Tamar's voice was gentle yet persuasive.

Elisheva faltered. "Do you — do you think you can?"

"I sure do." Tamar grinned at her. "Shall we have a go at it?"

Elisheva smiled back at Tamar's use of the South African turn of phrase. "Sure." She went over to the table and sat down. "Let's!"

Nearly three hours later, they were still struggling. Tamar's usual patience was eroded by her exhaustion. Yawning repeatedly, she tried to explain it again.

"Look, Elisheva. Just write that doing something because of *ahavah* is infinitely greater than doing it out of *yirah*. See, it says in '*Va'eschanan*' thousands of generations next to the word '*ahavah*' and just one thousand near the word '*yirah*.' Get it?"

"No," Elisheva mumbled.

"Just write it, okay?" Tamar yawned again, so widely she thought her jaws would crack.

"Sure. Sure."

It was after two o'clock before they finally turned in for the night. Elisheva's paper was nearly finished; she just needed to write it out neatly and make sure it was well-organized. They fumbled themselves into nightgowns and collapsed into bed.

"Tamar?"

"Hmm?" She was already on the verge of sleep.

"Tamar...thanks. I couldn't have done it without you."

Tamar managed to crack one eye open and smile tiredly. "You're welcome, Elisheva. Good night."

Shani stared out the window of the car, rubbing the misted glass impatiently with her glove. Despite the lighter Sunday traffic, it was slow going on the icy streets of New York. Dr. Baum drove with caution, his foot hovering over the brake, as they turned into the underground parking lot in the back of the office building.

With a sigh of relief, Dr. Baum turned off the engine and set the hand brake. "Well, Shani, we made it." He turned to smile at his daughter. "Let's go inside. At least it will be warm in there."

"Great." Shani smiled at her father as she slid out of the car, clutching her Chumash folder in her hand. It would be several hours before they would go back to Bloomfield; Dr. Baum's office was always full on Sundays. She planned to finish her paper in the office and get it rewritten before it was time to go back home.

Father and daughter entered the imposing lobby and made their way to the elevator, joining the waiting crowd. "Daddy?"

"Yes, Shani?"

"What did Mr. Kaplan say when you told him I was coming?"

Dr. Baum gave Shani a sharp glance. "Actually, he seemed rather surprised that you were aware of the situation, but once he heard that Rochel had given you her approval, he had no objection."

"Oh." Shani rubbed her thumb against the edge of the folder. "Were — were *you* surprised that I know?"

"I suppose I was." A soft chime sounded and the elevator doors slid open. They held back for a moment while several people walked out from the elevator, then followed the crowd inside. "Can you reach the buttons, Shani? Number five... What was I saying? Oh, yes. I was a little surprised. You may not realize it, Shani, but Rebbetzin Falovitz apprised us of Rochel's situation before she came."

The doors slid silently closed, and the floor rose beneath their feet. Shani blinked at her father with surprise. "She did? How come Mommy didn't tell me?"

Dr. Baum's brows drew together as he frowned down at her. "Because the Kaplans made it clear that they don't want anyone to know, Shani. And even if they hadn't been specific about it, we probably wouldn't have told you anyway. Why would it have been necessary?"

"Um, yes, well..." said Shani, her voice trailing off.

Dr. Baum's face softened. "It's all right. You do know now, after all, and Rochel doesn't seem to mind your being here, so I suppose it's worked out for the best." The elevator came to a smooth stop on the fifth floor, and they stepped outside as the doors opened. "I hope you're careful not to speak about it to anyone else, though."

"Oh, sure. I've never said a word to anybody, not even Tamar and Elisheva. And I don't really discuss it with Rochel, either."

Dr. Baum shot her a glance as they walked down the hall to his office. "One day, you'll have to tell me exactly how you found out..."

Shani had no time to reply as they walked into the waiting room. The place was empty, save for the Sunday receptionist behind a window and one mother and child who had come earlier than expected.

"Good morning, Mrs. Cohen," Dr. Baum said genially to the woman sitting on one of the upholstered chairs. "If you let me get washed up, I'll take Dovie in right away." He gave his daughter a final nod before disappearing into the consulting room, closing the door quietly behind him.

Shani settled herself as best as she could in one corner of the waiting room, laying her folder on the low table in front of her and pushing the magazines aside.

Dr. Baum's consulting hours on Sundays were from one to four. Rochel might come in any time after three. It was now ten minutes to one.

Shani sighed and opened the folder. It was going to be a very long wait.

Eleven

Rochel stared across the kitchen table at the cool, willowy girl seated opposite her. Leah Malka's eyes were green and impersonal, sweeping everything with the same measuring, steady gaze. She was not pretty in the usual sense of the word, but her face had character, hinting at a strong personality lurking just beneath the surface. There was something in her, too, of her father: a subtle sensitivity, an innate understanding of when it would be best to retreat. That insight had certainly proven to be invaluable in the last twenty-four hours…

Mr. Kaplan, arriving at the Baums' home five minutes before noon, had spoken little on the drive back to New York. They were only twenty minutes away from the Kaplan home before he broached a new topic.

"Rochel, I know this isn't easy for you. Your absence has left a gap in the house. Your mother misses you, your brothers miss you…and I, too, miss your presence. It would mean a lot to me, Rochel, if you thought of Leah Malka and Dovid — and myself — as family." He paused. "We are your family now, you know. It's been almost a year and a half. Your brothers have, *baruch Hashem*, adjusted very nicely, Rochel — we just wish you would be able to, as well."

Rochel had said nothing. He spoke nicely enough, but what did it really mean, anyway?

"Well," Mr. Kaplan said after a moment or two of silence. "I would like to ask your opinion of something."

Rochel bit her lip and stared out the window a little harder.

"You've picked up quite a bit of first-aid, Rochel, just by listening to descriptions of my work in Hatzalah."

"Yes," Rochel admitted grudgingly.

"I'm sure you realize how crucial it is to be proficient in the basics of first-aid and CPR."

"Yes," Rochel said again. She did realize. She knew her stepfather to be intelligent and skillful, an expert on both dealing with accidents and helping the victims and their families to cope with crises. She admired him for it, too. She just wanted to admire him from as far away as possible…

"Well," Mr. Kaplan said after another moment, "we have started giving voluntary CPR and first-aid courses in many Bais Yaakovs and yeshivos in the Brooklyn area. *Baruch Hashem*, we have had a very warm response from the students."

"That's nice," Rochel said after another minute or two. She couldn't help feeling a twinge of uneasiness. What was he leading up to?

"Rochel, Rebbetzin Falovitz called me earlier this week."

"She did?" Rochel squeaked, a thread of panic crawling over her.

"Yes. She wants us to initiate a CPR course in Bloomfield."

Rochel swallowed hard. "Are — are you coming to conduct it?"

"Well, no, I'm not. That wasn't a question in the first place." The car turned onto the quiet side street where the Kaplans lived, moving slowly as they searched for a parking space. "We usually have a woman conduct the CPR classes for girls. No, there's a different question. You see, Rochel, Leah Malka usually conducts the classes for Bais Yaakov girls."

"Leah Malka?"

"Yes. Leah Malka has known how to administer CPR since she was your age, and she's given classes many times. If it wouldn't matter to you, she would come teach the course. However..." Mr. Kaplan glanced at her in the rear-view mirror. "If you would prefer it otherwise, Rochel, there is another woman, Esther Gold, who works as a nurse. I've already discussed the possibility with her, and she seems willing to come out to Bloomfield to teach the course...if you would prefer it that way?"

Rochel drew a long, shuddering breath, her eyes blinking hard. "Yes," she managed to say, keeping her voice level and even by the sheer force of her will. "I would prefer it that way. I appreciate it. Thank you." *Thank you. I wouldn't want my stepsister in Bloomfield. Thank you for realizing that.*

As she followed her stepfather into the house, Rochel found herself admitting that Shmuel Kaplan was a very decent man. He had taken the time to consider her view, to realize she would be uncomfortable and embarrassed to have Leah Malka come and conduct a course in Bais Yaakov of Bloomfield. She respected him for that — but she still wished he wasn't married to her mother.

The entire Shabbos had been tense, a tightly coiled wire that would have sprung apart at the slightest provocation. Everything served as a painful reminder of her father — the singing, Kiddush, even the questions on the parashah that Mr. Kaplan asked Rochel's younger brothers. It was similar, agonizingly similar, but it would never, *ever* be the same again.

And Leah Malka? Rochel didn't know what to make of her. She was pleasant enough, and intelligent, but she held herself in a reserve that made Rochel keep her distance. At the same time, Leah Malka seemed to recognize that Rochel, too, had her own boundaries, certain lines that could not be crossed. The two of them, in unspoken agreement, maintained the reserve that they both demanded.

Now, on this Sunday morning, as the two girls sat together at the kitchen table, Rochel felt drained and exhausted. If her mother had hoped that she would relax and feel more comfortable after a Shabbos spent at home, she was in for a great deal of disillusionment.

Leah Malka stirred her coffee and added a generous dollop of milk. "You should come more often, Rochel."

"Oh, yes?"

"Oh, yes." The green eyes assessed her. "This is your home, after all. Or should I say — *our* home."

"Maybe." Rochel shoved her chair away from the table with more force than necessary. "Maybe not."

"No, Rochel." Leah Malka placidly raised her cup of coffee to her lips. "No maybes about it." She sipped her coffee. "It's just as hard for me to accept a new mother as it is for you to accept a new father. Maybe even harder; think about it for a minute. But that's not the point. We all care about you, Rochel, and we'd all like to see you back home. Why wait until Purim? Come home next week."

"Forget it," Rochel said shortly. "But thanks for the invitation." She stalked out of the kitchen and upstairs to her bedroom — her own, not shared with Leah Malka. *Baruch Hashem* for that!

A pair of green eyes, touched with a hint of regret and resignation, watched the younger girl walk off. With a sigh, Leah Malka picked up her cup once more and drank a mouthful of coffee, her face blank with remembering her own sorrows and grief.

Give her time. Eventually — hopefully — she would come around, and the festering wounds would finally get a chance to heal.

Mr. Kaplan slammed the car door shut, locking the car and withdrawing the key in one smooth motion. He reached over to pick up his stepdaughter's bag, but Rochel backed away.

"I can carry it myself," she said quickly. *Don't help me. Don't do anything. Let me keep myself whole.*

Mr. Kaplan's green eyes, so like his daughter's, regarded her thoughtfully. "Whatever you'd like, Rochel," he said quietly. "Shall we go in?"

Rochel followed her stepfather slowly as they walked out of the echoing stone building. Now, at the moment of truth, she regretted her initial decision. Did she really want Shani to meet this man? Did she really want her Bloomfield persona to meet the dark tragedy of her New York life?

It was too late now. Rochel's stomach twisted with nervousness as they approached the gleaming glass and chrome facade of the imposing medical building. In just another few minutes, she and her stepfather would enter Dr. Baum's office, side by side, with Shani's hungry, probing gaze fastened on them.

There was no way out…

"Oh! You're Hatzalah? You're in Hatzalah?"

Mr. Kaplan, a reassuring figure in his Hatzalah jacket, whirled around at the panicky gasp. A half-hysterical mother came toward them with jerky steps, holding her son's arm tightly. The little boy, wailing loudly, pressed a tissue, saturated with blood, against his lower lip, his eyes spilling over with tears of panic and fear.

With three swift strides, Mr. Kaplan reached the frightened woman and her son, bending down over the frightened child. "What happened?"

"He fell down the stairs," the woman said, her voice rising. "He knocked out a tooth…another one is loose… I need — oh…"

"Relax. He'll be okay." Mr. Kaplan straightened. "Who's your dentist?"

"Dr. Baum. Dr. Binyamin Baum." The woman looked dazed, incapable of thinking coherently.

"Come along, then," Mr. Kaplan said, his voice smooth and calming. "I'll come up with you." He reached down and took the boy's hand, guiding the frantic pair toward the bank of elevators.

Rochel watched them go, a trickle of relief easing the tension in her muscles. Let him go ahead, then. Anything to prolong the inevitable moment when Shani would gawk at them both.

Shani looked up hopefully for the hundredth time as the outer door swung open, then sagged back into her chair at the sight of a stranger — the mother of a boy who had finished some time before.

"Hi, Eli. Ready to go?"

"Yeah, Mommy." The boy struggled into his jacket and followed his mother out the door, giving Shani a cursory glance as he went.

Shani drummed her fingers impatiently against the armrest. Here it was, ten to four already, and Rochel had still not come yet. The last of Dr. Baum's patients had already left. What could possibly be taking so long?

Dr. Baum's Sunday dental assistant came out of the consulting room, put on his coat, and left. Silence enveloped the office, an oppressive, almost depressing silence. Office hours were over; the room seemed to settle, hunkering down in stolid patience for tomorrow's appointments. There should be no more noise, no breathing, no restlessly shifting patients sitting on thinly upholstered chairs. The Baums ought to be on their way home by now. Shani felt intrusive, blundering in where she didn't belong. Why didn't Rochel show up already?

Then a muffled sound came through the door. A high, thin sound that it took Shani a moment to recognize — the sound of a child screaming.

Even as she leaped to her feet, the door burst open again. Three people entered the room: an obviously distraught and half-hysterical mother; a wailing, panicky child with a bloody tissue pressed tightly to his mouth; and a tall man with cool green eyes, wearing a Hatzalah jacket and somehow radiating an aura of comfort.

"All right, Mrs. Ellison," he was saying reassuringly. "Doctor Baum will take a look at Yanky. We might be able to save those two teeth."

Dr. Baum came striding out of his consulting room, his eyes alarmed.

"What happened?" he demanded even as he bent over the child and gently lifted the gauze pad.

"I met them down in the lobby," the man replied succinctly. "Yanky here fell down the stairs. Mouth lacerated. The bleeding is stopped, Binyamin, but his front teeth are loose."

"Mm hm." Dr. Baum straightened. "Come in with me, Shmuel. I want to hear more details." He turned to the mother. "Mrs.…?"

"Ellison. Sarah Ellison," the woman said in a quivery voice.

"Okay, Mrs. Ellison. Do you want to come in, or would you rather not?"

"I think… I think…"

"I think you should sit down," the man whom Dr. Baum had called Shmuel suggested gently. "We'll call you in soon."

"No…no, I want to stay with Yanky…"

Mrs. Ellison followed the two men as they took Yanky, now only whimpering, into the inner office. Shani, her eyes alive with curiosity, followed, pausing in the doorway where she knew she wouldn't be intruding. Eager to watch the drama, straining to see exactly what was going on in the small office, she nearly jumped two feet in the air when someone tapped her on the shoulder.

"Hey! You awake or what?" Rochel, still bundled up in her padded winter jacket, looked at her with some exasperation.

"Rochel! I didn't see you come in!" Shani whirled around, quickly scanning the waiting room in her hope of finally meeting Rochel's stepfather, but Rochel had apparently come in alone. That was strange. Didn't Mr. Kaplan have to pick up dental equipment from her father?

"Yeah, I noticed." Rochel grinned and leaned against the wall next to her, but Shani thought she detected a wary look in her eyes. "What's doing?"

"Nothing much. My father's working on a patient right now. This lady came in with her kid and a man from Hatzalah."

"Uh *huh*. I know."

"You what?"

"I said I know." She straightened up to peer over Shani's shoulder. "Is the kid okay?"

Shani stared at her, puzzled, before turning back to watch too.

The small room was crowded. Mrs. Ellison stood near the dentist's chair, her fingers fluttering with anxiety. Dr. Baum's fingers probed gently in Yanky's mouth, while Shmuel, the man from Hatzalah, gently but firmly held down the boy's flailing hands.

Dr. Baum, glancing up at his tray of sterile instruments, caught sight of the two girls standing in the doorway. "Shani, out," he ordered curtly as he chose one gleaming tool from the tray. "Stay in the waiting room." His gaze softened as he turned to Mrs. Ellison. "It would be better if you waited outside, too, Mrs. Ellison. We'll call you in soon."

Shani backed out almost gratefully, swallowing hard against the taste of bile in her mouth. She wasn't all that used to the sight of blood. Rochel, on the other hand, seemed calm and relaxed as she sat down next to Mrs. Ellison.

"He'll be okay, Mrs. Ellison," she told the woman

reassuringly. "They're going to splint the teeth so the roots can continue growing in the bone."

Shani blinked with surprise. How would Rochel know that? Come to think of it, Rochel had shown medical knowledge before. And how could she possibly be so calm about so much blood?

Mrs. Ellison looked bewildered.

"That means they're probably going to be able to save his teeth," explained Rochel.

"Oh, I hope so. My poor Yanky...he got so hurt when he fell...he was crying so much... He just slipped on the ice and fell down the steps outside our building — seven steps. He banged his mouth so badly, and —"

Rochel nodded understandingly, her face a study of interest. Shani marveled at her poise as she listened to the stream of words pouring out of Mrs. Ellison's mouth. This was exactly what the woman needed most right now: somebody to listen, to talk to, to get her mind off her eight-year-old son whose mouth was getting stitched up even as they sat here. How did Rochel do it?

Twenty minutes later, the Hatzalah man appeared in the doorway to the inner office. "All right, Mrs. Ellison," he said cheerfully. "Would you like to come and take a look at Yanky, teeth and all?"

The woman jumped up. "Oh, thank you, thank you! I was so worried, I —" Her voice faded out as she disappeared into the little room.

The man stood there, eyeing Rochel and Shani with that cool gaze. "Everything all right?" he asked.

"Sure," Rochel replied. Shani looked at her with surprise. "No problem."

Dr. Baum, coming out of the office with Mrs. Ellison and Yanky in tow, overheard Rochel's answer. "I see you train them well, Shmuel," he chuckled. He spared a glance at Shani. "I wish *my* daughter was as knowledge-able about my work."

"Your daughter? Your —" Shani goggled at Rochel, then at Shmuel — Shmuel Kaplan. Rochel's stepfather!

Shmuel Kaplan regarded her calmly. "Are you interested in first-aid, Shani?" he asked.

"Y-yes," she stammered. "It's very important to know."

"How would you feel about taking a CPR course?"

"I'm sure I'd like it," she floundered.

Rochel cast her a look of amusement, knowing how rarely Shani found herself in an awkward situation. This time, however, the discomfort was of Shani's own making. "Yes, I'm sure you will."

Dr. Baum turned to Mrs. Ellison. "Yanky's going to have a sore mouth for the next few days, but he'll be all right. The sutures can come out in five days' time, and —"

Shani didn't listen any further. Dazedly, she walked to the other end of the waiting room and sank into a chair. She didn't know what she'd expected Rochel's stepfather to be like, but she sure hadn't expected him to be anything like this.

Mr. Kaplan went back into the inner office with Dr. Baum to discuss the equipment to be donated to Hatzalah. Rochel and Shani stared at each other, their expressions twin mirrors of studied neutrality, neither one daring to speak.

Rochel and Shani avoided the issue on the long ride back to Bloomfield. They spoke about safe, general topics: the upcoming performance in Rollenton, the assignment that they'd both completed, the Purim Festival the elementary was planning. It was only after they arrived in Bloomfield, when Dr. Baum had walked ahead of them into the house, that Rochel faced Shani belligerently.

"Well?" she demanded, her voice daring Shani to voice her opinion.

Shani considered her, trying to make out her expression in the fading light of rapidly approaching dusk. "You've learned an awful lot from him," she said finally. "He must be very good at helping people."

Rochel's face changed, her brown eyes becoming thoughtful. "Yes," she said slowly. "You're right. I did. And he is."

Twelve

Monday morning, five days after they'd handed in their assignment. Eyes brimmed with hope, hungrily following the papers being passed from hand to hand. Swift intakes of breath, long sighs of relief, and soft sounds of happiness rustled through the classroom.

"Rivki Kuperman." Twenty-two pairs of eyes focused on the fair-haired girl as she walked tremulously up to Rabbi Levi's desk. He smiled reassuringly as he gave her back her assignment. "Well done, Rivki." Rivki's face sagged with relief, and she walked back to her seat with wobbly steps.

"Rochel Kaplan." Rochel, last on the alphabetical list in Hebrew, had long since grown resigned to the aching, gnawing suspense of being the last one to give a presentation or receive a corrected paper. She stepped forward, and Rabbi Levi handed her the last of the checked papers. "Very well done, Rochel. I enjoyed your topic."

As Rochel sat back down, Rabbi Levi rose from his desk, coming around to the front. "Your grades are all high, which reflects the work you've all done. And may I remind you, ladies, that I grade each of you individually according to effort. I would not recommend you bother comparing marks." He gave them an ironic smile. Most of them could not help smiling back. Rabbi Levi gave them the same speech every time he corrected an assignment or a test.

"In general, girls, I was highly satisfied with your work. You showed initiative and effort, and I was particularly pleased to see that most of you did not choose subjects you had already learned. I saw a willingness to learn, a desire to do this work because it interested you, not just because you had to." Rabbi Levi's dark eyes settled on Elisheva, whose paper had merited a high grade. "Elisheva, your paper touched on this point. Would you like to clarify it?"

Elisheva paled. She had no idea what Rabbi Levi was talking about. "I-I don't think I could explain it so well anymore." She gulped.

"I see." Rabbi Levi leaned back against his desk, steepling his fingers, his eyes thoughtful.

A cold fist of dread closed around Elisheva's stomach. If Rabbi Levi realized just how little she understood of her own paper...

"Perhaps someone else could help us out here — Tamar? How about you?"

Tamar blanched, turning as pale as Elisheva. "I think Rabbi Levi is talking about how the reward for a mitzvah done out of love is much greater than a mitzvah done out of fear." Her voice was low and strained.

"Yes, Tamar, that's exactly what I'm talking about." Rabbi Levi straightened, pacing slowly down one of the aisles. "Because you girls made the effort to do this project with enthusiasm, not just to fulfill the minimum requirement, you have all gained a great deal. You can be proud of yourselves, girls. I'm certainly proud of you." The bell rang at that moment. "Class dismissed — Tamar and Elisheva, can you stay behind, please?"

The ninth graders filed slowly out of the room, an undercurrent of uneasiness drifting alongside them like a choking fog. Something was wrong. Something had happened, something with Tamar and Elisheva — but what?

As the classroom emptied, the two boarders hesitantly approached the front of the room. Tamar's thudding heart was working overtime as she realized what she'd done without even being aware of it: the *mefarshim* she had explained to Elisheva, the lessons in *hashkafah* she had practically dictated to her roommate at two o'clock in the morning, were nearly identical to those of her own paper. Rabbi Levi, with his sharp eye and astute mind, had noticed the similarities. What was going to happen to her now?

A voice echoed in her mind, a voice that sounded vaguely familiar. *No. Cheating is* never *worth it.*

Could that voice really be her own?

Chana Hochberg, the last one out of the room, closed the classroom door softly behind her. Elisheva and Tamar stood before the teacher's desk, the condemned standing before the judge and awaiting sentence. The silence grew and grew, until it threatened to choke them both.

"Do either of you have anything to say?" Rabbi Levi asked gently, looking from one girl to the other.

"No," Elisheva said simply. "I don't. I was wrong. I apologize."

"I see." His dark eyes moved to hold Tamar's own. "Tamar?"

Tamar swallowed. "We — we didn't mean to cheat, really. I just tried to help Elisheva out a little. She mostly understood it on her own…" Her voice faded out.

"Except for that point that I mentioned in class?"

Tamar lowered her eyes. "Well…we were sort of tired at that point. I guess I just told Elisheva what to write." She sneaked a look at her fellow roommate and partner in crime. Elisheva just stood there, her back straight, her head held high, her gaze level. How could she do that? How could she accept the embarrassment and humiliation with such poise, such dignity?

"I see," Rabbi Levi said again. He tapped a finger on the desk. "Am I to understand, then, that Tamar wrote one and a half papers?"

"Yes." Elisheva's voice was still clear and firm. "I was wrong."

"I didn't *want* to just dictate," Tamar said helplessly. "It's just that — that —"

"Tamar, I do understand that it is difficult for you — both of you — to be living away from home. You are coping with a challenge that the local girls do not have to deal with. In the end, though, it would be best for each one of you to make a mark based on your own abilities."

Tamar bit down hard on the inside of her cheek, trying to stop tears from welling in her eyes, while Elisheva absorbed the rebuke calmly, her incredible reserve unshaken.

"Elisheva, what do you think should be done now?" Rabbi Levi turned a hand over. "How do you think we should resolve this situation?"

Elisheva took a deep breath. "If Rabbi Levi is willing to give me a second chance, I will write another paper on a different topic."

Rabbi Levi nodded slowly. "Very well, Elisheva. I will give you until Pesach to write another paper."

"Thank you," she said softly.

The elementary principal regarded the two girls for a moment longer, then stood. "All right, girls. In that case…"

"But, Rabbi Levi, I *am* trying," Tamar said desperately. This couldn't be happening. It couldn't! Her favorite teacher disappointed in her, after she'd worked so hard on her assignment? "I'm trying to make my own mark here. I have a get-together every Shabbos with the fifth-grade girls on *shemiras halashon*, and I'm even helping Chaya Leah…"

The look on Rabbi Levi's face stopped her in mid-syllable. "Yes," he said, his tone expressionless. "You do help Chaya Leah. However, we are discussing schoolwork now, not other issues."

Tamar closed her eyes. She couldn't look at her teacher anymore. With that one blurted, fatal sentence, she had irrevocably destroyed any last vestiges of good opinion Rabbi Levi had ever had of her.

She heard his voice echo strangely in her mind, as if he were speaking to her from far away. "You'd better run along, girls. The next bell will ring any moment now."

Tamar kept her gaze fastened to the floor, refusing to look at Elisheva or meet the curious glances of her fellow classmates, standing just outside the room. She said nothing, not a word, as she slowly walked away, stepping carefully to avoid trampling on the shattered, broken shards of her own self-respect.

"Shani, you've got to do something." Chana Hochberg's face was strained and desperate. "Half of our performance depends on Elisheva. She's in the dance and the band and she's got a solo. She can't drop out on us now!"

"Well, what am *I* supposed to do?" Shani waved her hands helplessly. "I've tried talking to her. She just gives me this sad little smile and shakes her head."

Chana groaned and buried her face in her hands.

"This is really serious, Shani." Michal Elias paced in a circle, her forehead creased with worry. "The performance is in just two weeks. We can't go start all over again from scratch. We need Elisheva."

The three girls were holed up in Shani's bedroom. Chana had been shocked — horrified, even — when Elisheva had come up to her at lunchtime and told her that she was dropping out of the band choir. Repeated and increasingly frantic appeals had shown no results, and they had come to Shani's house to try once more before giving up completely.

"Look, I'll try to talk to her. But I don't think it's going to help." Shani grimaced, kicking moodily at the edge of her bed. "In fact, we can all go down and try to talk to her. She's not going to listen, though."

Somberly, the three girls went downstairs, through the kitchen, and down into the basement. Rochel wasn't home yet; she was still at the Newmans'. Tamar sat on her bed, her face expressionless as she stared unseeingly at the open pages of her notebook. Elisheva sat at the table, surrounded by a sea of *sefarim* and notebooks.

"Can we talk to you, Elisheva?" Shani asked tentatively.

"Sure. If you'd like." Elisheva's face looked drawn, her delicate features strained and tired.

"It's about — the band choir."

"Oh. I'm sorry, Chana, but I have to do this." She looked at the open Chumash in her hands. "I-I messed up this assignment, and Rabbi Levi is giving me a second chance. I'm not going to waste my second opportunity. I'm sorry, but I'm not going to play music again until this is finished."

"But you're letting us down, Elisheva." Chana couldn't stop a pleading note from creeping into her voice. "What are we going to do?"

"Don't you understand?" Elisheva demanded, her cheeks growing red as she jumped to her feet. "I don't want to do this. I want to be able to play. But I *can't*. I have to do this, whether I want to or not." She slumped into her chair, the flush slowly fading. "Maybe next time, Chana. I'm sorry..."

"Yeah." Chana straightened, her eyes angry now. "I'm sorry, too." Without another word, she turned and stamped upstairs, with Michal following behind.

Shani lingered for a moment longer. "Can't we change your mind, Elisheva?" she asked softly. "There's no need to do this, you know. Maybe you were at one extreme before, when you spent so much time practicing that you didn't have time for classwork. But you don't have to go to the other extreme now and not play any music at all. Just in moderation, Elisheva. A little bit of each..."

For a moment, Elisheva wavered, torn by her desperate longing to be able to join the band choir, to play the music she loved and win the respect of her friends. Just her half hour of practice. That wouldn't be so terrible, would it? She half-turned in the direction of her flute case — and caught sight of Tamar sitting on the bed, her face still white and her dark eyes devoid of their usual life, the happy sparkle of polished onyx dulled to rough obsidian.

Elisheva stiffened. *She* had done that. If she hadn't succumbed to the temptation of easy assistance, Tamar would not be miserable right now...

No. She deserved to suffer, as she was causing Tamar to suffer.

"I'm sorry, Shani," she said, her soft, lilting voice firm with determination. "But my decision is final."

In the days that followed, Elisheva discovered just how much she'd always depended on that precious nightly half hour of music. Each evening, as eight thirty approached, Elisheva found her feet moving of their own volition toward her flute case, her fingers curling into position as if they held the precious instrument in their grasp. It was an almost physical pain for her to turn away, to retrace her steps back to the table and sit down once more with her books. More than that, she found herself growing nervous and edgy; she had no privacy, no music, nothing to help her relax and soothe her nerves.

The sudden drop in temperature of her relationship with Tamar did not help matters. Tamar avoided her as much as possible, concentrating on her precious fifth graders. Elisheva was unsure if Tamar was actually angry with her, or if this over-exuberant girl from Kedzie felt that Elisheva was angry with *her* for helping her in the first place. For that matter, Elisheva wasn't sure how she felt about it, either...

The treatment she received in the classroom, however, was the worst. Nobody said anything out loud, no one actually accused her of betraying the class, but the eyes — the eyes that followed her every move, the eyes that flicked over her with cool contempt, the eyes that slid away from her when she tried to meet someone's gaze — the eyes said more than enough.

Why didn't anyone seem to understand what she was doing? Why was she struggling against a tide of misunderstanding?

More than anything else, she longed to snatch up her flute and lose herself in music, to forget the world around her and soar with the intricate melodies of her beloved classical music. But she herself had closed that door. Until that assignment, newly completed, was handed in to Rabbi Levi, Elisheva would not allow herself to touch her precious flute.

Rochel watched Elisheva torturing herself for several days before she finally got exasperated enough to say something.

"Elisheva, this is ridiculous. What makes you think you're supposed to drive yourself crazy? If you want someone to drive you insane, I'll be glad to volunteer, but you don't have to go and do it to yourself."

"That's not what I'm doing," Elisheva argued. "It's just that I've made a commitment with myself, and I'm going to keep it."

Rochel threw her hands into the air with disgust. "Trust you to make a commitment to make yourself miserable!"

Elisheva swallowed her retort with an effort. She wasn't interested in fighting with Rochel, any more than she wanted to be fighting with Tamar and Chana and the others in the class who were treating her so coldly.

Life was lonely enough. No need to make it worse.

Thirteen

amar hummed to herself as she slid the cookie
sheet with its neat rows of fortune cookies into
the oven. It had taken her hours of preparation,
and she felt a fierce sense of satisfaction in knowing that
she'd finished a long and complicated task.

She walked downstairs to the room, trailing her
hand absentmindedly along one wall. She had the
Baums' house to herself; Rochel was at the Newmans,
Shani was at practice, Elisheva was working in the Bais
Yaakov library, and Mrs. Baum had taken the younger
kids shopping. She wasn't Elisheva, but she did relish a
moment of privacy from time to time. She may as well
enjoy it while she had the chance.

She knew her fifth-grade girls would enjoy the game
she'd created for them — eating the fortune cookies,

finding out which girl had the second half of the halachah of *shemiras halashon* written on the small slip of paper inside, then acting out a two-minute skit based on that halachah for the rest of the group. Creating the "fortunes" to put into the cookies had taken her the longest, of course. She had to copy out the *halachos* from *Guard Your Tongue*, divide them in half, write them on tiny scraps of paper, and insert them carefully into the fortune cookies. Now, all she had to do was keep an eye on the clock and take them out when they were done.

Her eye lit on the fat book lying on her pillow. She had a few minutes. Why not…?

Tamar's eyes devoured each line of the page as she read with rapt fascination. She rarely had the opportunity to sit down and read, much less a new book she'd never seen before. Now, however, with the fortune cookies baking in the oven, she had some time…

Half an hour later, Elisheva mounted the steps and dug her key out of her pocketbook, juggling half a dozen notebooks at once. She was so *tired*. More than anything else, she wanted to collapse in a quiet room and play music; but her paper for Rabbi Levi still had a long way to go, and Elisheva refused to give in to temptation. Until she finished the assignment and handed it in, she was just going to have to suffer.

Elisheva turned her key in the door, surprised to see that it was already unlocked. She pushed open the door, walked inside, took two steps, and froze. A terrible smell, riding on a wave of black smoke, poured out of the kitchen.

"Is anyone home?"

There was no answer, but the smell grew stronger. Elisheva fought down a surge of panic. She had no idea if she should run out of the house, call the fire department, or do any one of a hundred things. She backed away a little and yelled as loudly as possible.

"Is anyone home? Something's burning!"

Then she heard it — a faint cry of dismay coming from the basement, then pounding footsteps sounding on the stairs.

"Oh, no!" Tamar lunged for the stove and opened the door, sending fresh billows of smoke boiling outward.

"What is it?" Elisheva coughed, staggering into the kitchen.

"It *was* my fortune cookies…" Tamar pulled the cookie sheet with its blackened lumps of char out of the oven and tossed it onto the counter. "Somehow, I don't think the kids will find it very appetizing." She eyed the little black masses, wisps of steam escaping from the centers — the burned slips of paper, no doubt. She made a face as she scraped the burnt cookies off the cookie sheet and into the garbage. Elisheva, bemused, watched Tamar tidy up somewhat perfunctorily from the disaster.

"There!" Tamar looked around the kitchen. "As good as new — well, almost anyway. Not my cookies." She sighed, then gave Elisheva a rueful grin. "Oh, well, back to the drawing board!" She turned and headed downstairs.

"Back to the drawing board?" Elisheva repeated as she followed Tamar into their room. "What's that supposed to mean?"

"It means I'll have to start all over again," Tamar replied. "I mean, do I have a choice? They sure can't eat those cookies the way they are right now." She walked over to her bed and picked up the fat book lying on the floor, where she'd thrown it in her wild haste to rescue her cookies. She made a face as she straightened the bent and creased pages. "I guess I deserve it, though. I started reading and I totally lost track of time."

Elisheva sank into a chair and stared at Tamar, almost awed. "I simply do not understand you."

"Why?"

Elisheva opened her mouth, then closed it again and took a deep breath. "You've spent hours making those cookies. I saw you working on those little fortunes yesterday. Now they've gone up in smoke — literally — and you're going to have to start all over again. You make dozens of phone calls, work during all your recesses in school, use up half of your after-school hours to prepare activities and songs... Why, Tamar? Why do you drive yourself mad over this?"

She stopped abruptly, startled at the words she had just said. Why did they sound so familiar?

What makes you think you're supposed to drive yourself crazy?

Hadn't somebody told her that, not so long ago?

"Mad? Oh, you mean crazy... Well, I'll tell you why," Tamar said soberly. "This is what I do. This is what I am. I work well with little children; I always have. If I couldn't do what I do best, I'd feel like I'm only half a person. And I'm just lucky enough that what I'm good at is helping others... How could I possibly give that up?"

Elisheva stared at her. "But..." she whispered. "But that's how I feel about me. About my music."

Tamar shrugged. "Then don't stop playing. We've all noticed how miserable you've been, Elisheva. Don't torture yourself like that."

"But — my Chumash assignment. I have to concentrate only on that." Elisheva sighed, slumping into her chair in a manner most unlike her usual erect posture. "I wish I could do it differently, but music and Chumash just don't go together..."

"What are you talking about?" Tamar demanded. "Don't you know that David HaMelech is called the Sweet Singer of Yisrael? And how about the Levi'im in the Beis HaMikdash? And how about —"

Tamar stopped short and turned away, a bitter smile twisting her mouth. She was doing it again — pushing her way into Elisheva's business. She'd had enough of that already. They'd both suffered as a result. Enough was enough.

"I'm sorry," she muttered. "Just forget I said anything. I don't —"

"Tamar?"

Tamar turned around. Elisheva's expression was unreadable — a mixture of hope, nervousness, and tentative courage, all at once.

"Tamar, is there a topic I could use from Chumash that has to do with music?"

A slow flush of joy flooded Tamar's being. Maybe, just maybe, this was her chance to try again with Elisheva — to help her, but stay within the limits. To lend assistance without taking over. To be a friend…

"There sure is," she said softly. "Can I help you get started?"

"I'd love that," Elisheva answered, her voice equally soft. Then her face grew impish. "Unless you want to get started on your fortune cookies first…"

Tamar gave her a startled glance, then burst out laughing. She was still chuckling as she pulled down a *sefer Shemos* and sat down next to Elisheva, reforging a closeness she had feared would be forever lost.

…you probably realize how surprised — let's say shocked — I was to get your letter.

After all, we don't really know each other yet. Maybe we should try to know each other better, though I still have my doubts about that. I'm willing to listen, though, which is more than I was half a year ago.

Rochel chewed thoughtfully on the end of her pen.

Maybe this is better than a phone call, or even a visit home. After all, with a letter, you can't —

"Rochel?"

Rochel glanced up from her notebook. Shani's voice. "Yeah?" she yelled back.

"Can I come down?"

"Sure, go ahead."

Footsteps sounded briskly on the stairs and Shani came down the steps and into the room. "Where're Tamar and Elisheva?" she asked, looking around.

"Not here, as you see." Rochel waved a hand. "I'm not their mommy, so I don't really feel the need to make sure they're home by five o'clock every afternoon."

Shani grinned at her. "You're in fine form today."

"Why, thank you. Anything I can do for you?"

"Well, sort of." Shani twisted her hands around each other. "You know how Elisheva backed out from the performance?"

"Sure. Everyone knows about that."

"Did you try to make her change her mind?"

"Yes, but so did everyone else in the class. Why do you ask?"

"Well, I want her to come with us to Rollenton. Maybe she'll change her mind at the last second."

"Sounds a little far-fetched to me, Shani, but if you want to drag her along, go right ahead. Why come and discuss it with me first?"

"Because I want you to come, too." Rochel started to say something, but Shani spoke faster now, trying to muster all her arguments before Rochel could object. "We need you there, Rochel. We want everyone to be there. The whole class. It's not the same if it's not all of us. You know what I mean. *Achdus* means the whole class working together, and you may not have noticed, Rochel, but you're part of the class, too." Shani took a deep breath. "Please come along. Say you will. We want you to."

Rochel blinked. "If you put it that way," she said slowly, her voice sounding strange, even hoarse, "I guess I have no choice."

"So you'll come?" Shani leaned forward, her blue eyes hopeful.

"I just said I would, didn't I?"

"Oh, Rochel! Thank you!" She leaned forward and hugged the New Yorker impulsively. "Oh, I just know this is going to work out. You'll see!" She darted back up the stairs, her blond hair bouncing with excitement.

Rochel stared after her, bemused. She was wanted. She was needed. Part of the group…

Well, maybe, anyway. It was a start, she supposed.

Shaking her head, she bent back over her notebook, continuing the first draft of her reply letter to Leah Malka.

Tamar trudged upstairs and into the kitchen, rippling a sheet of paper between her fingers. With a worried frown, she ran her eye down the list of fifth graders. Fraydie, Malka, Shevi, Bracha, Shosh, Simie, Devora, Estie, Nechama — she'd called them all. The only girl she still needed to call was Chaya Leah Levi.

Tamar consciously stilled the tremor in her fingers. Since that horrible confrontation, she hadn't needed to call the girls at home. This time, though, she couldn't wait until tomorrow to pass on the message. She needed to call the girls tonight and make sure they would all be able to come.

But how — *how* — could she possibly call Chaya Leah Levi, the principal's daughter?

It wouldn't be a problem if Chaya Leah picked up the phone; if her mother answered, or any of Chaya Leah's eight brothers and sisters, that wouldn't be a problem, either. But Tamar dreaded the thought of dialing that number and hearing Rabbi Levi's deep voice on the other end of the line.

She'd already blundered once by dragging Chaya Leah's name into a discussion where it didn't belong. What if Rabbi Levi felt that she was trying to win points, trying to squirm back into his good graces after her *faux pas*?

The alternative was unthinkable. She couldn't just ignore Chaya Leah. While the fifth graders were slowly, gradually adjusting their thinking, she could still sense resentment simmering somewhere deep below the surface. Until the girls' residual anger had subsided completely, she didn't want to give them any opportunity to snub Chaya Leah, or even a chance to talk about her when she wasn't there. She *had* to come to this activity.

Tamar took a deep breath, commanding her churning stomach to behave itself as she lifted the phone and began to dial. Her stomach didn't listen.

One ring. Two rings. *Please don't be Rabbi Levi,* Tamar thought fervently. *Please don't be Rabbi Levi. Please don't —*

"Hello?"

A deep, vibrant voice. A man's voice. Rabbi Levi's voice.

She almost hung up the phone, then and there. Then she dragged together the remaining shreds of her equilibrium. She could just ask for Chaya Leah. She didn't have to say who she was.

"May I speak to Chaya Leah, please?"

"She's not home right now. Can I take a message?"

Tamar almost cried. Should she or shouldn't she…

"This is Tamar Bergman."

There was a pause on the other end of the line. "What can I do for you, Tamar?"

"Well, I'm —" *Get on with it*, she told herself. *You're committed now.* "I'm having a *shemiras halashon* activity at the Baums' house tomorrow, straight from school. I wanted Chaya Leah to know about it today so she could get permission to come."

She held her breath, waiting. Waiting to be reproved, to be censured, to be warned against currying favors.

"I see." Rabbi Levi paused again. "As Chaya Leah's *father*, Tamar, I can tell you that I'm very pleased about the *shemiras halashon* group that you've formed with the fifth graders. I can actually see an improvement in their speech and their behavior. I will certainly pass on the message, and Chaya Leah definitely has my permission to go."

Tamar groped for a chair and sat down. "Thank you," she managed. "Thank you very much."

"You're welcome." Tamar could almost see Rabbi Levi's smile. "Juggling public and private selves isn't always easy, Tamar, but I think you can manage it."

"Thank you," Tamar said again. She couldn't think of anything else to say.

"Thank *you*, Tamar. Have a good day."

Tamar slowly hung up the phone. She knew she was grinning — a pretty foolish grin, too — but she couldn't help herself.

As Chaya Leah's father…juggling public and private selves isn't always easy… I think you can manage it…

Whistling a tune slightly off-key, Tamar waltzed across the kitchen and downstairs to the basement. She knew, with absolute certainty, that everything was going to be all right.

"Shani!" Chana shrieked over the line. "Elisheva just called! She's back in the choir!"

"Calm down," Shani ordered, grinning. "You're breaking my eardrums."

"Sorry," Chana apologized, her voice more moderate. "I'm just so relieved. We'll have time for one more good practice before we leave, so it works out just right." She paused for a moment, her voice changing further. "I guess we owe her an apology, though. We weren't very nice to her… Do you think she'll accept an apology from us?"

Shani looked at the girl sitting next to her, with her small, delicate mouth curved upwards in a faint smile. "Oh, I think she'll accept the apology," Shani said into the telephone, winking at Elisheva. "I think she'll accept."

The CD player fought for supremacy with the electric organ in the back seat, while laughs and shouts drowned both out entirely. Bashie Klein, eyes intent on the road, ignored the bedlam to the best of her ability as she drove the large, lumbering van along the expressway toward Rollenton.

Elisheva sat right in the middle, squashed between Rochi Davis and Raizy Segal. She felt almost drunk on happiness as she blew a triumphant chord on her flute.

"V'heishiv lev avos, lev avos al banim…"

"I'm so glad you changed your mind," Raizy told her softly. "Not for us, Elisheva — for you."

"Yes, you're right." Elisheva's light-blue eyes seemed a deeper color than usual in the relative dimness of the van. "I don't think I would have been able to, either, if Tamar hadn't helped me find just the right topic for my Chumash paper."

"Oh? What topic?"

Elisheva leaned forward and whispered in her ear, and Raizy laughed aloud.

"Perfect, Elisheva. Absolutely perfect!"

"I know," Elisheva said softly. "I know."

For the twenty-three members of Bais Yaakov High of Bloomfield, the trip to Rollenton was a dream come true. They greeted the girls who had come to Bloomfield for the *chidon* earlier in the year like long-lost relatives, and the Rollenton girls welcomed them with equal enthusiasm. They were divided into five groups and sent to five different homes, where they had a chance to rest and wash up after the three-hour drive from Bloomfield. And later that night, when the performance was over and they were suffused with the warm, tired glow of knowing they had done well, Elisheva remembered the thought that had flashed through her mind the day the concert was first proposed: *Perhaps she couldn't make her mark with classwork, but she had confidence that she could do well in any situation that called for her music.*

She had done well for herself; in her music, in her classwork, with her friends.

Maybe America wasn't so bad after all.

Epilogue

abbi Levi came to Bais Yaakov a little earlier that morning. He had no classes to teach, with the high school girls off in Rollenton, but he wanted to use the opportunity to take care of the paperwork that piled up to the point where he could barely see his desk. He nodded a "good morning" to Mrs. Jeworsky, the secretary, as he collected notes and mail from his letterbox and carried them to his inner office.

So many papers, circulars, notices… With a methodical eye, Rabbi Levi sifted through the rustling piles of papers, making a pile here, discarding sheets there, putting questionable papers over here…

He lifted a memo from one of the elementary teachers, revealing a large manila envelope underneath.

Curiously, Rabbi Levi picked it up, opened it, and tilted it downwards.

Six neatly typed pages slid out into his right hand. The corners of his mouth tugged upwards in a smile as he read the title:

Shiru LaShem Ki Ga'oh Ga'ah
Miriam HaNeviah leading *bnos Yisrael*
in dance and song

by Elisheva Conrad

Coming Up Next in B.Y. High

A question of survival…

Will Rochel be able to use her skills to save a person's life?

Can the new high school survive a tragic disaster?

Is this the end of B.Y. High?

Find out in B.Y. High #3: *Going Home*!